CAS~~SANDRA'S WAY~~

BOOK ONE OF THE MAGICAL

WAYS SERIES

BY: YASMINA KOHL

Yasmina Kahl

DEDICATION

There are so many people I have harassed, harangued and tortured in the creation of these stories. Yet despite it all, they are still hanging around.

The first and with the largest "oh my God you're still here" award goes to my husband, "ACDC" :) These stories are completely and one hundred percent his fault. Okay fine, be that way, the first one is his fault, the rest of them are all on me, and the evil plot bunnies that say, "Hey you, should write this."

The next 'omgysh' award goes to my kids, Chris and Nikki...though come to think of it, really why are you still here? Shouldn't you be, you know, graduated or something?

Then there are all the people who have egged me and the evil plot bunnies along: Kelly, Katrina (the pain lady), Eric, Jennifer, Don, Tami, Homer & Elizabeth, Dave, Kelly, (yep there is more than one) and the most evil of them all, Stuart. Also can't forget the one who named me; Mikey, your copy is in the mail. Wink wink nudge nudge.

Cassandra s Heart

Then there's Jeff, Cheryl and Jessica, and crap I'd have to write another story just to list everyone.

Also I have to add a hello to a couple of furbabies who are not with us anymore, Gabriel the Amazon Bitch Cat from Hades, and Buddy the Black Lab/Chow who killed four vacuum cleaners in 12 years without attacking a single one. And yes, the cat actually existed. Now for the furbabies who are still here, Shadow and Wren...stay off my DAMN KEYBOARD.

I also want to thank the people from The Collins Inn, The Able House, The Poulson Museum and Capitol Treasures for letting me wander around their buildings in search of the best hallway. I want to thank the Tokeland Hotel who had the absolute perfect hallway, even though I'm not using the photo any longer.

INTRODUCTION OF CAST AND CREW

To a casual passerby, Magical Ways is a high-end clothing boutique. To its employees and customers, however, it is a family, a good one. Okay, yes, dysfunctional, but there is fun in dysfunctional after all.

The owner, Yvette Lacroix, comes from an intriguing heritage. Her mother grew up in Louisiana just outside New Orleans. Her family has been there for more generations than anyone could be bothered to remember. The Lacroix's are a huge family; many of whom are well versed in voodoo. Now, they are no Madam Laveau, but then who is?

Yvette's mother is a high priestess and a well-known herbalist in the area.

Her father, Martin Marchi is from the Bronx. New York Italian all the way and as if to add to the cliché, his family has more cops in it then mobsters.

This is something that has always made them proud. At Marchi family get-togethers, there are more brass shields than most small town police departments could dream of having.

Cassandra s Heart

One might ask how a beat cop from the Bronx got together with a voodoo priestess. Mardi Gras… it took Martin one trip to the Big Easy and all of his vacation time to get Anastasia to agree that they were it for each other, followed by weeks of expensive long distance phone calls begging her to come back to New York to live with him. When she finally agreed he was ecstatic.

When she gave in months later and agreed to be his bride, he walked on air for a week. When she asked him to take her name instead, he balked for a moment, but in the end, what did a name matter? Sure, the guys at the precinct would give him hell for months, before and after the wedding, but what did he care? He had the thing he wanted most in his life. The man born

Martin Marchi became Martin Lacroix in the name of love. Out of that love, was born Yvette. And we'll just say that Martin's life was never dull.

The first to come to Yvette's new self-picked family at Magical Ways was Cassandra St. James. Yvette's family being what it was enabled her to understand the young empath and her need for a calm, caring, and understanding environment. Cassandra was well loved by her parents and her mother's triplet sisters. She met an amazing man, and Mark helped her when her mother died, and then again within the year when her father was lost to a broken heart. But it was the aunts, Grace,

Monica, and Tabitha that had to try to keep the empath sane and healthy, when Mark was killed in an accident- not an easy task.

Anne Simpson was second to the family. A woman of small stature but a giant in demeanor, her Robert called her "my queen." As with any well-loved queen, he denied her nothing. They had their sorrow though - the sorrow of not having children. They redirected this love and compassion into helping the young people Robert found at the shelter where he volunteered. He always found someone to bring home with whom they could share their lives until the young person was able to stand on their own and move on, thanking the couple for their help. Anne and Robert had both been only children and like Cassandra, were both orphans, losing their parents shortly after reaching adulthood.

Melissa Carter came next. She was the most outwardly different person of the family. She had several piercings in each ear, eyebrow and a small nose piercing. Her style was gothic, yet somehow didn't offend Magical Ways clientele. She changed her hair color often, but never in the usual hues. No, Melissa used the entire rainbow as her palette. Customers actually came in more often just to see what Melissa had done this week. Melissa, had secrets like everyone does, but some of hers were a little bigger than the others.

Melissa had come from California looking to get away from her 'family'. A connected family, and it was the connections she feared. Her father had been a mob enforcer and when he was killed, his boss took her in. Aniello raised her, but his lifestyle wasn't what either of them had wanted for her so she left while it was still an option.

The final and littlest sister to join their fun-yet-dysfunctional family was Emiko Nara. Emiko was shy, lost. Cassandra had once described her as a single leaf caught in a tornado trying to keep itself from being shredded by the sheer force around it. Yvette thought that was an astute description. Emiko had been sent to The States as punishment for something that had never been in her control.

As the boys came into the Magical Ways family, it grew by leaps and bounds.

The first to come was James Austin, a horse trainer and a grounded, no-nonsense guy who needed a little magic in his life. James works at the Double L. He comes from a large family with three sisters, both his parents, all of his grandparents and assorted cousins as well as aunts and uncles.

Xavier St. Cloud stumbled into their group next. Xavier had seen better days, and the battered war veteran was on an edge. Either he was going to get better or he was going to die. He preferred the latter, but everyone around him seemed to prefer the first.

Johnnie and Christian Castelo are twins, one good, and one trying to be good. Johnnie had started out on the wrong side of the law, but his brother had worked hard at getting him straightened out and keeping him straightened out.

Christian was a damn good architect. Where and whenever possible he used Johnnie's construction company for the projects he designed.

Leo Evens more or less sauntered into their mix. Leon is a jack-of-all-trades, but mostly he tends bar or acts as a bouncer. He was a loaner by choice, having been stabbed in the back more than once, metaphorically and physically.

Josh has worked with James Austin for a while now but still kept quiet about his life. In his line of work, his secret could get him seriously hurt if not killed. He was excellent with the horses and even better with the paper work that went with them. He's known Cassandra for many years but after his cousin, Mark's death, their relationship faded into nothing.

Alexander Jackson was a grifter who literally had a second chance beaten into him. He cheated the wrong group of people and paid for it. Steve and Jack, the officers who found him clinging to life after the attack started looking after him and helped him realize that if he didn't change he was going to die. He liked living so decided to try change. Now instead of tricking people to survive, he lives by saving people. His secret is not bad for his current situation, but it has gotten him hurt in the past, and he's hoping it won't again.

CHAPTER ONE

Cassandra walked through the park scattering breadcrumbs for the birds. She wandered with no thought about where she was or where she would end up. Mentally she wasn't anywhere near the park or her body, but lost in her own thoughts of misery. She silently called to Freya, her goddess. *'Please, I know you have never been one to help the weak and timid, but I need someone else to be strong now. I just can't seem to manage it anymore.'* She vaguely felt the stranger's gaze follow her. She didn't want to think about anything other than trying to get past the pain in her chest but still there was a pull to look in his direction. She resisted looking for as long as she could but in the end, she couldn't stop. What she saw was a ruggedly handsome man staring back, with eyes of the deepest green. 'Freya I'm not looking for a new love, just the ability to get past a lost love.' The wind swirled around her trailing her long coat in the man's direction. "I said no," Cassandra whispered to the wind. She intentionally turned the opposite direction from the man and walked out of the park.

James watched the tall brunette stroll aimlessly, feeding the birds as she walked. She looked as lost as he felt. He continued to stare at her unable to look away. The very air around her seemed to crackle and sizzle with…something… energy maybe? Wherever the woman walked, the leaves stirred around her as if she was the wind. To continue her odd aura, there seemed to be a ground fog flowing around her. The tails of the red paisley scarf she wore trailed behind her just a little as the wind continued to swirl lightly around her.

Guessing, James placed her close to his own height of six feet. Her hair was a beautiful shade of brown. It hung down to the middle of her back in casual waves with red highlights showing. Her profile showed her nose had a little upturn at the end, and her chin was what James figured would be termed classical.

Not wanting to miss anything, he begged his body not to blink. He watched her smile slightly, and then bow her head, turning away from him.

James was about to follow her but felt a hand on his shoulder. "Escaping the ranch, cowboy?"

He looked up and found his ex-girlfriend looking back. "Beth, what… wait, what?"

"Articulate as usual I see."

"Yeah, yeah, sorry. What are you doing here, Beth?"

"Just taking a walk…don't really want to be at home. Mom's up for the weekend."

"Ah. That will do it."

"Definitely."

James knew Beth and her mother did not get along. The two loved each other, but they mixed as well as gas and fire...there was bound to be an explosion.

"Look, I'm gonna head back, training a new colt. He's shy, and it's a pain. It was good to see you again Beth. Really it was."

"You could always come back with me." Beth said with a suggestive tone and a glimmer in her eyes.

"No, Beth, that part's over."

"Can't blame a girl for trying."

"Nope, I can't." James said walking off in the direction the brown-haired woman had gone.

Having been with James for 18 month as a couple and for years as friends, Beth had seen how James acted when he was into a girl. "Damn, she's got him, and neither of them even knows it," she thought.

***

A few hours later Cassandra was in the stock room of Magical Ways Clothing Boutique, sorting the new inventory that had come in.

"Where are the sweater sets? Damn it, I need one for Aunt Grace. Mary's birthday is coming up. Damn it."

"Muttering to yourself again dear?" Anne inquired.

Cassandra looked up to see her coworker walk in to the store room, "Yes, the sweater sets, where are they?"

"On back order, they will be here in a couple days. Plenty of time for Grace to pick one up for her friend. Does that woman wear anything but sweater sets, by the way?" referring to the friend of Grace's that she had only met once but the meeting had left a deep impression.

"Only to bed." Cassandra said with a shudder.

"Thanks for that mental picture." The short clerk mirrored Cassandra's shudder at the thought of Grace's friend in lingerie.

"You're welcome."

"Bitch." Anne said heartlessly.

"No witch, get it right."

Taking the bull by the horns, Anne asked the question everyone had been skirting for months. "So honey, when are you going to move on?"

"What?"

"It's been a year." Anne asked, knowing Cassandra would realize she meant Mark's death.

"I know how long it's been."

"I'm sure you do darling, right down to the minute, but you need to move on. You need to pick up your life and, well, pick up a man."

"Anne, I love you dearly, but while I may be at the moving-on stage, I am not yet at the picking-up-a-man stage."

"Yes you are. You need to be."

"What do you mean I need to be?" Cassandra asked bitterly.

"You need love and affection. You are dragging, we can all see it. You have dark circles under your eyes, you've lost weight, you're pale, you don't come out with us any more, you stay home with no one to keep you company but your pets. When was the last time you enjoyed a girls' day with your aunts? I may not understand as much as Yvette or Melissa when it comes to you and your empathy, but I know you need to keep your shield up with laughter, love, and happiness. If you are hiding from places where these emotions are abundant, you are going to kill your internal battery. And if I understand, it'll just about kill you."

Cassandra sat on the floor fidgeting with the stock before her. She knew all of these things, had lived with the requirements of her "gift" for years. She could only keep up the shields that kept other people's emotions to a soft whisper using her own energies for so long. If she kept going the way she was, she could injure herself permanently, and in a worst-case scenario, she could get sick enough and die.

"Cassandra darling, we all love you, we want you to be happy. We understand that you needed time, but darling, you have to look out for yourself. We need you as much as you need us. You're our big sister. All that aside, you are the only one who can reach the damn labels when Yvette's off." Anne's feeble attempt to make Cassandra laugh worked and Cassandra let out a quick chuckle.

CHAPTER TWO

It seemed to James that he just couldn't stay away from the park this week. Sparks was driving him crazy. The colt just kept losing focus, and of course, so did James. Maybe if the trainer could focus, the trainee could, too. James thought if he took a longer break from the colt he might be able to focus on other training methods for him. James didn't know why he felt so scattered.

Boss was an understanding person; he knew animals, both the two and four legged versions. He knew that the four-legged kind didn't always mesh well with the two-legged kind but given enough time, they might. He would give James the time he needed.

Still thinking of how to train the colt to be the exceptional wrangling horse James knew he could be, James didn't notice the brunette from that morning walking towards him lost in her own thoughts. The inevitable happened, and they collided.

"Oh, I'm sorry."

"I'm so sorry, I didn't see you." Cassandra apologized without looking up.

"Oh, it's you."

"Last time I looked." Cassandra said nonchalantly.

"I saw you this morning. You were here feeding the birds."

"Yeah, I saw you with your girlfriend."

"An ex-girlfriend much to her displeasure."

"Oh."

Trying to get a conversation going with the beautiful woman James asked, "Do you come here very often?"

"Only when I need to think."

"Oh." James said crest-fallen "I should leave you alone then."

Not wanting the man to leave, Cassandra said, "No, no it's okay. I don't mind. I just didn't want to go home right now."

"Someone bothering you at home?" he asked, hoping no one was hassling this beautiful woman.

"Just myself."

James noticed the mist was around them. A funny thing though - it wasn't cold enough for there to be any ground mist forming. Shaking off a weird buzzing feeling he asked, "Would you like to go somewhere, and, I don't know, get a cup of coffee or tea or wine, whatever?"

"I have wine at my house."

"Thought you didn't want to go home?"

"It doesn't sound so bad if someone else is going to be there."

"It's up to you."

Cassandra decided and asked the cowboy. "Do you want to follow me in your car?"

James shrugged, "Had one of the hands drop me off, was just killing time. Trying to think some work stuff through."

"Alright, I'm parked over there." Cassandra pointed over her shoulder in the direction she had come from.

James followed Cassandra through the winding paths of the park all the while watching the eerie mist follow them and spill in front of her. One thing kept rolling repeatedly in his head. Why was he following a woman he didn't know to her car? Why did he keep coming to this park? He worked on a ranch- it wasn't like he couldn't get enough outdoor time at his nine to five, and since he started coming to the park six months ago he had he always sat in the same place and did the same thing. Had he been waiting for her?

"What's your name?" he asked.

"Cassandra. Yours is James."

"Huh?"

"Your jacket." Cassandra stopped and pointed to his tattered and worn letterman's jacket, which had certainly seen better days.

"Yeah, guess that would be a dead giveaway wouldn't it?"

"Yep. Here's my car." She walked up next to a cherry red convertible.

"Nice."

"It's a fuel cell hybrid."

"Nicer. I put a diesel motor in my Jeep so I could use biodiesel. All the trucks on the ranch I work at use biodiesel."

"I like your ranch already."

"Then I bet you'll like this even more -we make about a third of it at the ranch."

"I do like that. I don't use enough oil to make my own."

"Consuela cooks for all the hands, so we use quite a bit of oil. And one of the hand's wife is the manager for a little taco stand so we get their oil to."

"Good. So what kind of ranch is it?" Cassandra asked, pulling out of the park into traffic.

"We train horses for all kinds of uses."

"Not a farm then?"

"No, Consuela grows some spices and a few veggies, but to grow enough to feed the crew would be a full-time job, and the guys couldn't care less where the food they eat comes from so long as there's plenty of it and it's hot."

"Ah."

"The only reason we even use the biodiesel is because Boss's wife had a fit when she realized how much gas we used. Boss told her he didn't care, but after she showed him how much cheaper it was to switch." James shrugged.

"First year costs were higher 'cause of selling a couple gas trucks and buying diesel ones, but since then we only spend a thousand or so in fuel 'cause all the machinery is diesel, too."

"See, if everyone did that, it would be so much better."

As the two lapsed into a surprisingly comfortable silence, James looked at Cassandra. She'd rolled her window down, and the wind caught her hair so that it flowed behind her as she drove. The passing streetlights lit her face. Her profile was strong and drop dead gorgeous to James. He had seen her eyes earlier when they reached her car; they were the same bright and clear blue of the seas he'd seen in photos of the Caribbean. She honestly did look like some temple goddess who had stepped out of a relief or a carving and had come to life.

"Do you know how exquisite you are?" He hadn't meant to actually ask the question but it was already out there.

"I guess," was her reply. Cassandra knew that others thought she was beautiful but to her she was just, Cassandra. She did like her height, it helped to be tall working as a manager of a clothing boutique. You can always reach items your customers can't.

James wondered how a woman so beautiful didn't know it.

"Here we are." She pulled up to a section of apartments towards the back of the complex and parked at the end. From what little of Cassandra he knew, he guessed that the apartment with the flowers at every window and along the small walk, was hers. He was right. She walked over, picked up a black cat, and opened the door, and then he found out why she hadn't bothered to unlock the door. "This is Odin and Freyja."

Odin was a large Irish wolfhound. No one would dare enter the apartment without his permission. James wasn't sure he wanted to either, but after one loud bark that seemed to proclaim, "All here is mine," he sat down and just watched. "He's a big pussy cat. Really he is." Reaching down and roughing up the calico's fur, "She on the other hand is the one you have to look out for. I call her my Amazon bitch cat from Hades." With that, she dropped Freyja to the couch and walked to the kitchen.

CHAPTER THREE

James looked around and took in all the sights. There were hundreds of books scattered everywhere, boxes of incense with names from freesia to dragon's blood. Knives and swords adorned the walls where there weren't sculptures of men's faces made of leaves, as well as fairies and other figurines on the wall that he just couldn't make out with the lack of light.

"Do you like fruit wines?" Cassandra asked, but James merely shrugged.

"I make it myself; I pick the fruits in the summer and freeze them. Then in the winter I make the wine." She handed him the glass of wine and laughed at his expression after the first sip. "Sorry. Maybe I should have warned you, I spike it with enough Everclear to make you sit up and take notice." Cassandra shoved Freyja off the couch knowing that the demon cat would never willingly give up her spot for anyone, including her mistress. "Sit down."

James was instantly smashed after one good swallow. He sat down, watching the cat to see if it would attack, since his ass was sitting in the spot she had just warmed. "I like this, it's good. It's a little strong for my normal drinking palette, though."

Until this moment, Cassandra had only been thinking about not being lonely another night. She had family she could call for company. Any one of her three aunts would have been there at a moment's notice, but she didn't want the three weird sisters. She didn't know how, but she had done what Anne had wanted. She had somehow without knowing it moved past Mark's death and was working towards, well horny. She chuckled to herself. Had she been "trolling" for a man and not even known it?

"So your um, uh, décor is a bit different from most places I've been."

"I'm pagan."

"Huh?"

"Easiest way to say it is to say I'm a witch."

"Wait, like devil worship and all that?"

"No, like I believe in the gods that were worshiped long before Christ came out of the sands of Mesopotamia."

"Huh?" James brain stopped as he tried to figure out what Mesopotamia had to do with the devil.

"Iraq, Iran, Israel and all the Middle Eastern countries were at one time part of Mesopotamia. Christ came from the same place as Allah. I believe in the Norse gods. Odin, Freya, Thor, Loki and the

rest. They have had followers
for generations before a monotheistic religion was ever conceived of."

"Okay, I think I get it." After a long pause James shook his head and said, "No, wait I don't. What's that got to do with the devil again?"

"Satan is purely a Christian idea. There was no Satan until there was Christ."

"Okay."

"Can't worship what didn't exist." Cassandra explained.

"No, don't suppose you can."

"Pagan used to mean country dweller and when the Christians started taking over Rome it was slanted to mean someone who didn't believe in the new way, the 'only' way. Now it means someone with a polytheistic view, with less of the slander slant."

"'Kay, what's polytheistic?"

"Someone who believes in more than one god."

"Okay." James said understanding the new term.

They sat in silence for a while drinking the wine. Slowly James drank, knowing damn good and well it was going to slam into him shortly. He just wasn't good with booze. Tonight seemed to be a little different though. He was buzzed but more than that, he was horny. After the initial confusion with the whole pagan thing, the only thoughts running around his head were how to get home to get rid of the monster in his jeans. He wasn't about to sleep with this wounded bird the first night he knew her. She just seemed too damn vulnerable. Of course, the more he drank the less he was sure he could keep that promise.

Cassandra reached over and touched James's hand to get his attention, "So what do you think of being in the lair of a witch?"

He looked up from her hand to those eyes again. They were just so damn perfect. However, this time he saw something he hadn't noticed before: lust and sexuality. His heart flip-flopped in his chest. "Do I have to answer that right now? I have only seen your living room." And god or whoever, I hope to see more, ignoring the thoughts I just had about not sleeping with her.

"No, I don't think you have to answer right now. I can show you the rest of the place if you want." Cassandra was thinking that maybe a grand tour of her apartment would be enough to calm her feelings. The next time she thought about seducing someone, maybe she should drink the other wine. Not that there had been any planning in tonight's seduction.

"Sure, I would love to." James was wondering if the whole place would be decorated with the same whimsical/magical motif. And he found that it more or less was. The kitchen was a pale blue, the bathroom was a soft purple and the shower curtain had a forest scene on it. The next room-a study or extra bedroom, he wasn't sure-was in a bright sunny yellow with even more books and candles and all of them looked handmade.

Then there was the Master Bedroom. He was surprised because it was so different from the rest of the house. In it was a large four post cherry wood bed with a canopy of rich burgundy velvet. The comforter was a dark midnight blue; the satin sheets looked to be a shade lighter. The walls were a muted grey that without the rich jewel colors of the bedding would have made the room look like it belonged in a hospital.

"I love it!" James exclaimed. "It's wonderful." All the furniture in the room matched. The dresser had been carved with a floral motif and was made from the same deep red cherry wood. The nightstands on either side of the massive bed were the same as was the dressing table near the window.

He suddenly had a flash of her thirty years from now at that table putting her hair up...it had only slightly turned silver. He shook his head. That kind of thing had never happened to him before. He felt all tingly. James was still trying to shake off the feeling without her noticing.

"I'm glad you like it. It was my great-great-grandmother's. Her father was a wood carver in the old country and when she was born, he started making it for her as a wedding present. It took him 27 years. She married later in life because her fiancée was a trader and was gone on long sea trade routes. When he was made captain, his company was opening an office in America. He got the posting and everything they owned was brought over."

"She was very lucky." He reached over and ran his hand down the post of the bed.

"Sit down." She smiled knowing that it was what he wanted to do, but was too much of a gentleman to just sit down on a lady's bed without being invited.

He sat down, grateful, because the alcoholic effects of the wine were beginning to hit him. She sat down next to him and drained her glass. Not wanting a woman to think she could "drink him under the table" even if it was her wine, he did the same. Within seconds, he knew that had been a terrible idea. It went straight to his head, but not the one on top of his body.

Cassandra had also noticed his reaction to the wine. She never figured herself to be a conniving person, but she knew he had to be extremely hard by now. He had already admitted that he was a lousy drinker. Cassandra knew her reaction and his too for that matter - were because of the wine, but she just didn't care. There was no threefold law for followers of Freya, even so Cassandra believed in the Wiccan Law that what you do comes back to you with three times the force. She leaned over to him and slowly kissed his cheek, moving closer and closer to his mouth, placing her hand on his leg. She could feel the heat rising from his body.

She was on fire from head to toe. She was so wet and ready for this. The wine helped but only in the smallest of ways. She didn't want to stop but wanted so much more at the same time. "When did he take off his coat or when did I take off my sweater?" All she knew was that his shirt had to come off NOW!

Cassandra pulled his shirt free from his belted 501's, dragging her nails lightly along his skin so that he hissed. She broke the kiss only long enough to pull his shirt off.

James was burning with desire. He had always been the one to make the moves in the past, but Cassandra, she said she wasn't like other women and now he knew for certain that she meant it.

He couldn't wait for her to reach his mouth, so he turned his head towards her and their lips met and he felt another tingling sensation. He slipped his tongue in just a little and she accepted.

Their tongues danced a dance that was older than any of her gods. He broke the kiss to pull her in to his lap. Then he began kissing her neck and nibbling on her ear. He didn't remember either of them taking off her sweater, but as he brought his hands down to her shoulder, he felt only her silky skin. Running his fingers over her arms and around to her back was heaven. "The gods must have made you…no mortal could have done this well."

James whispered into her mouth just before he kissed her again.

James couldn't believe how he felt. Okay, it was cliché, but he had never felt this way before. He grabbed her back as soon as his crumpled shirt hit the floor. As he kissed her, he worked to free her breasts from the violet satin bra. As her bra fell away, Cassandra leaned in to James but felt him retreat slightly. She broke the kiss and looked at him. "What?" Cassandra said in a voice husky with lust.

An image of angels in red leather popped into his mind. Damn angels. He wished they would go away; he just wanted to be left alone with the wanton witch sitting on his lap. He knew she was ready and wet. He could smell her musk; he could feel her warm dampness through his jeans. "It dawned on me that we just met," he moved so he could see her bedside clock, "an hour and a half ago."

"I know...but it feels much longer doesn't it?"

"Yes, but why?"

"Because we are...soul mates." She had paused over the term soul mates, but found it sat better with her as she said it and heard herself say it.

As he heard her say soul mates, the image of her sitting at the table came back. This time he could see his reflection in the mirror. He had more silver than she did, but time had been good to him, or at least in his imagination. He was sure she was right - how else would he have met this pagan beauty? It would seem there was very little chance of them frequenting the same places or having the same friends, but everything felt good, wonderful. "Yes I think we are. I have always believed in the possibility of love at first sight, but never could imagine how it would feel. When you said that, I know that I do now."

Cassandra leaned onto his shoulder and said, "I thought I had found it before, but I was wrong. I realized that twelve months ago. I lost my fiancée, Mark. He was killed in a car accident and for some reason today is the day I was, I am supposed to move on."

"I'm sorry about Mark. I'm sure he loved you very much."

"It just wasn't meant to be for this life." The whole time they had been talking, Cassandra had been running her hand over his chest and back.

James had been doing the same thing. Comprehending that they were both all right with what was turning out to be an extremely short courtship, as well as the whole soul mates thing, James began kissing her again with renewed vigor. Cassandra returned the kiss with equal energy. Hadn't she been tired earlier? "Must be the wine; it's mixed with ginseng." Cassandra reached down and unbuckled a well-worn leather weave belt. She fumbled a bit with the five buttons.

"Why did I wear these pants tonight of all nights', he wondered to himself. Because he hadn't planned to go to bed with anyone but 'Rosie', that's why.

Neither of them wanted to break the heated kiss. A kiss that had nothing to do with angels, no matter what color leather they wore.

CHAPTER FOUR

Finally, they had to break apart to remove the rest of their clothes. James fell to his knees so he could take Cassandra's skirt off. God, this woman knew how to pamper herself. The skirt was made of Egyptian cotton in a purple of unmatched richness. He tugged lightly and the skirt dropped from her hips to pool at her feet. James ran his hands down over her ass. He ran his hands over her thighs while he pulled her closer. Her scent was so strong, it was intoxicating. If he hadn't already been drunk from the wine, it would have been a great contact high. He grinned at that thought. He laid his head against her stomach. "You're so beautiful," he said again. He reached for her satin panties that were drenched with proof of her readiness. As he pulled them down, he was overcome with the sweet smell of her. He kissed her stomach all the way down to her milk chocolate hair. He tried to push her back so she would fall to the bed, giving himself better access to her core but Cassandra shook her head.

Murmuring a lust riddled, "No," she pulled him to his feet. Then she dropped to her knees and dragged the waistband of his jeans with her. His forest green boxers did nothing to hide his mammoth erection. He stepped out of his jeans and tennis shoes all in one move. Cassandra looked up at James; his eyes were so dark they looked like majestic fir trees in the middle of a storm. Sliding her hand up his leg to his shaft, she seized it. He hissed again from the heat of her hand. "Damn woman, I'm supposed to lead," he growled.

Cassandra had never enjoyed giving blowjobs and had honestly only done it twice before if truth was told, but with James, it seemed like it might be different. Slowly she took the crown of the head into her mouth. She smiled around his cock when he growled again.

A few minutes of her sucking his cock, James was beginning to get weak in the knees. Cassandra stopped and pulled him to the bed, but instead she ended up on the bed with James kissing her everywhere all at once.

"Not my time yet, little cherub," he whispered into her ear. "Ladies first, my mother always told me." James suckled her breasts and found heaven again.

He was beginning to think he was a religious man after all, but he sure as hell was not a man of the cloth. The entire time he spent nibbling gently on her nipples, his hands were never still. They roamed over her face, neck, shoulders, arms, and breasts. James moved towards the wet triangle of her pussy and Cassandra moaned. Slowly, not knowing how experienced she was, he started sliding his finger between her supple folds. Cassandra arched her back a little to meet him. James went a little further with each pass. He slid back up to kiss her again, never stopping his hand. He slid in a finger and rubbed her clit with his thumb. Cassandra arched her back again and moaned into his kisses, he added another and then a third and knew she was full. He knew he was just about that big. James moved his hand in time with her movements driving her towards her climax. "Oh the Gods be praised. That feels sooo good," Cassandra said as he began to thrash slightly, "MMM. Oh yes." If he kept kissing her, Cassandra wasn't sure she would wake from the bliss threatening to overtake her.

Then it did. She screamed into the night. James briefly wondered if her neighbors would mind. He didn't care anymore when she reached down and brought his hand towards her mouth and began sucking her juices from his fingers. That almost sent him over the edge. "Oh Cassandra! God woman, do you have any idea what that does to a man?"

"Mmmmmmaybe," she said with that wicked grin of hers. "Maybe."

"Remind me to thank whoever it is you worship when this is done."

34 | P a g e

"You already are. You already are." Cassandra knew James had to be close, he'd been close when she led him to the bed, and seeing her orgasm and then sucking his fingers couldn't have helped. She had calmed down enough to be able to think almost clearly. She rolled over so she was lying on top of him, she sat up and turned so she was facing his feet. She leaned down and picked up where she had left off; James nearly came as soon as her lips touched his cock. "Oh my god."

James was so close to coming, but he knew if he did that would be the end of this. Not that lying there next to her wasn't enough. It just wasn't enough right now.

"Woman you have got to stop doing that. You're going to send me to an early grave." He suddenly tensed up. Cassandra had already lost someone she loved, "How could I say something like that?" he thought to himself.

"It's okay…James…I'll play nice if you want me to," she murmured. "I've dealt with Mark's death; there was nothing I could have done. I wasn't even there."

"I just didn't want you to think I'm an insensitive jerk."

"I know you're not, or you wouldn't have tensed up." Cassandra leaned back down still playing with his balls, "Do you want me to play nice?"

"NO!"

"Good, 'cause I don't want to." She sucked one of his balls into her mouth and ran her hand up and down his shaft. That was all it took.

"OH SHIT." Now it was his turn to scream into the night, as he came, she took his shaft back into her mouth and swallowed it all.

A short time later he asked, "You don't have neighbors that you'll have to apologize to in the morning, do you?"

"No, I don't, they moved out last month."

"Thank you. I don't remember ever shouting like that. However, you are pretty vocal too."

"I know, I always am." Cassandra lay down next to James. As the two lovers curled around each other to bask in the glow of their new love, the moon rose higher into the sky.

As it reached its zenith, James turned to Cassandra and watched her sleep. He felt his heart swell and wondered if it could burst. He reached out and kissed her forehead like one might kiss a sleeping child. She stirred slightly turning her face towards him. In her sleep Cassandra murmured, "James." His heart stopped. After so few hours of knowing each other, she was thinking of him in her sleep. James kissed her slowly awake.

Her clear blue eyes fluttered open, seeing without seeing. She smiled when she finally focused on him clearly. He smiled back. Cassandra kissed him back in a way that woke up more than his mind. He nuzzled her neck looking for the spot all women had...that spot that drove them nuts. He smiled to himself when he found it, right in the crook of her neck and shoulder, she moaned. He nibbled on it for a few minutes until she was thrashing. He worked his way down to her breasts and suckled them for a while. Cassandra lay there, enjoying every bit of it. He had said "ladies first." Kissing his way to her pussy, he hoped she wouldn't distract him. "God her skin tastes good." He knew she would taste even better. He didn't want to rush this time.

Anticipation of sex for the first time in six months had not let him go slowly before, but he sure as hell was going to take his time now.

He reached her pussy and her musk was as sweet as it had been before. He leisurely kissed the inside of her thighs. Kissed all around her beautiful pussy, and slowly slid his tongue between her luscious folds. She quivered and moaned. He moved up and down her folds occasionally flicking the tip of his tongue over her clit, sending shock waves through her system. James pushed his tongue in farther and slid it back out. He kept probing further and further with each lick. Cassandra would moan occasionally, and she would suck her breath in as he flicked her clit. James marveled at this woman, did she ever end?

Cassandra was feeling the first waves of what she was sure would be an earth-shattering orgasm. She also knew that when she did she wanted him buried in her. "James, please, please" she pleaded. "I need to feel you, I need you."

"You have me, my sweet," he said, knowing full well what she meant, but unwilling to give up his pleasure quite yet. "I'm going to make you wait just a little longer." She sat up so she could see the devilish grin on James's face, covered in her juices.

"They say there is no devil...I think I might have just found him and proved them all wrong," said Cassandra with exasperation as she flung herself back on to the bed.

James went back to his pleasure and her torture. He knew she needed him soon, but not yet. He moved so he was sitting on his knees. James grasped Cassandra's legs and held them while he moved to plunge into her. He thought before he did that he should ask if she was a virgin.

"Cassandra, you have...?"

"Yes..." was all she could manage as he entered her and she climaxed. James had no plans of joining her anytime soon. James set a fast tempo and when she came back to earth, Cassandra matched it. After what seemed an eternity filled with several more orgasms for Cassandra, James finally joined her.

Several minutes later when James's brain was not completely fuzzy he asked, "What am I going to do with you my sweet witch?"

"Marry me someday." She said off-handily, not expecting the response he gave.

"Is tomorrow too soon?"

"Just a little," she stammered, "I think there's a license we have to get that takes two or three days." She barely managed to hide her smile and caressed his chest.

"I suppose I'll just have to wait."

"Maybe we should talk first?"

"Okay about what?" James asked with trepidation.

"Well I have a feeling you're more than James the horse trainer."

"Yeah, I suppose I am. Bet you're more than Cassandra the pensive pagan as well."

"You start."

"Okay. James Martin Austin, born and raised in a small town in Southwestern Washington, no one can find or pronounce. Moved here to train horses. I've always been in love with them but was never good enough with math to be a vet. Mom and Dad are still there, but I visit them a couple times a year. I'm the oldest child of four; never married, favorite color is blue. And yes, I know my name sounds like a car. Your turn."

"Cassandra St. James, born and raised here, manager of Magical Ways, a clothing boutique down town. Both parents are gone, only child, but have three aunts who stop by constantly. They seem to think I don't eat enough."

"You look good to me." James smiled as he ran his palm over her curves. His heart ached when he thought she had no family. At least she wasn't totally alone. "How long have...?"

"A couple of years. My mom had heart problems her whole life and when she went to the Summerlands my father followed her soon after. He couldn't live without her. Mark helped me a lot. When he went, I wasn't sure that I could go on, but my aunts and friends helped me so much."

"What is the Summerlands?" James asked, figuring it was heaven or her version of it.

"Heaven or something like it anyway. It's where you wait for your next life and where you go when you're done and are ready to move on to the next plane."

"Wow. Sounds great, when can I go?"

"Not till I go. I'm not doing the 'alone' thing again."

James hadn't mentioned a faith when he talked about himself, she could see no marks or jewelry that might tell on his gorgeous naked body before her. Plus today being circumcised had nothing to do with being Jewish.

Still intertwined in each other, Cassandra was feeling horny again and wanted him in her. She began sliding against his stomach just above his cock. While looking at him, she reached over and kissed him.

James was surprised. She had an appetite for sex that matched his and maybe surpassed it. He was even more surprised by the fact that he was damn near hard again. When had he ever been ready again that fast and for the third time in one night?

She could feel his cock coming to life under her leg. She knew he was a little surprised, she could feel it in his kiss. Maybe she should have mercy on his confusion and tell him about the wine? Thinking to herself, 'In the morning, I will tell him in the morning.' Now she would take advantage of its effects on the both of them. Finding she liked the taste of herself, Cassandra slid down and took James' cock into her mouth again. She wanted him rigid as a steel rod again and she was sure this would do it in a heartbeat.

James gasped as her hot mouth came down on his cock again. She knew how to drive a man to the edge with her mouth. He briefly thought about who had taught her and decided that he didn't want to know, not that he was jealous, he knew she had been with other men, at least one, she wasn't a virgin after all. He just didn't want to think about it. So he concentrated on what she was doing instead.

Cassandra felt him swell in her mouth almost to the point of gagging her. She slowed down so she could control the depth a little better. She didn't want him to know she had no idea what she was doing and was going on instinct alone. It helped immensely that he was so obvious about what felt good. She didn't think he even knew that he was doing it. Every time she hit a spot that must feel good, he would shudder, and this look would come over his face. She wanted to keep the look there permanently.

However, she had to have him now and hard. She wondered how he would react if she asked. Deciding to be bold and be a little demanding she did just that.

"James, take me, now, and fast." James was slightly startled by her demand but who was he to tell a lady she couldn't have what she wanted? "Hmmm, I don't know, I don't think you can take it again."

Then it was Cassandra's turn to be startled when he bolted up, quickly pinned her to the bed and entered her. She knew this is what she wanted; she wanted fast sex not love. James could tell she wanted it; she was writhing on the bed, matching his pace, and seeming to urge him on even faster. Well he would give it to her then. He wanted this night to be perfect, and perfect meant that she got whatever she asked for. He stopped only long enough to turn her on to her stomach and raise her ass up in the air, before reentering her.

She moaned in pleasure, writhing even more in this position. James could feel her muscles tightening around him and figured she was close to coming again. He hoped like hell he could stand it and not come himself because he wanted more of this. Cassandra was beginning to lose herself in the sensations she was feeling. She only knew what she was feeling but was unaware of her surroundings. Briefly, she thought to herself, 'This is pure sex, wish I'd had it before.'

Cassandra was so filled with sexual tension it scared her. Then without warning, she came so hard she nearly blacked out. All of her muscles contracted and convulsed sending a million sensations to James who came instantly. Both collapsed on the bed exhausted, neither moved for a very long time.

Sometime later Cassandra managed to say, "Maybe we should go and wash up. I don't know about you but I'm famished. So much sex."

"I could eat...after I shower." James answered.

Cassandra pulled James to his feet. She stepped into the master bath and it was like a tropical forest.

"Wow. Nice jungle you got going here!" Looking around the room there were several potted plants all around the medium sized room. He wasn't sure what they were but he could tell they were all healthy and had been growing for some time.

"Thanks. They love the steam from the shower. That and plants just seem to love me." She grinned. Cassandra turned to set the temperature for the shower and pushed James in.

"Wow, that's hot. I love a hot shower as much as the next guy but I also like my skin intact."

"It's invigorating. Besides, you save water this way. You can't stay in too long."

"No shit, you'd melt like ice on a lava flow."

"Oh it's not that bad." She added a bit more cold for his comfort. "I only have natural products and most of them are for women. Sorry."

"It's okay. So long as I can rinse off the sweat, I'll be fine." He took her soap from her and began washing her silken skin with it. "Now I know why your skin is so soft...it's your soap. It's as soft as you are."

"It has Shea butter in it, a moisturizer, and a few other things." She took the bar and returned the favor. When she finished soaping all the hard muscles of James's body, Cassandra washed her hair, then handed the bottle over her back to James, and got out while he finished.

He saw her work some cream into her hair and brush it out. He turned off the shower and stepped out.

"What is that? Beth, my um...ah... ex-girlfriend that is, well she had a hell of a time with her hair and it was only half as long."

"It's something my aunts make for me. They're herbalists. They could probably make her something if she wanted."

"She's my ex. Why would you offer?"

"Does she love you, do you still love her?"

"Uh, no and no."

"Then why shouldn't I? There is no reason we couldn't be friends."

"No, I suppose not. Just most people would disagree. But you're not like most people are you?"

"Nope. So what are you hungry for?"

"You."

"Thanks but I won't sustain you, just drain you." Grinning at him in the mirror.

"Okay. Cook's choice then."

"I think I have sandwich stuff." She offered walking into the bedroom.

"Sounds good to me."

"Good, come on." Cassandra threw a baggy plain black shirt at James and grabbed her robe. "Don't worry, it was my dad's. I keep it as a reminder of him. No matter how many times I wash it, it still smells like him."

Down in the kitchen Cassandra pulled bread, meat, and cheese from the fridge.

James sat on a stool at the breakfast nook. He watched her as she slathered the bread with mayonnaise and thought how beautiful her hands were.

"Hey, why a boutique?" he asked on a whim.

"Because I get a twenty percent discount." She giggled. "I'm a little vain, I like clothes, and I look damn good in them. Anyway, Yvette, the owner, is really cool and knows I have a weird life. She understands that I will work Christmas Eve if she gives me Yule and few other days off. She is very pagan friendly."

"Sounds great...my boss isn't quite that easy going." James picked up a giant sandwich stuffed with meat, meat, meat, and cheese. "How exactly am I supposed to eat this?"

"Tie a string around it like Shaggy and Scooby do."

James laughed, "That's cute, but I don't think it works in anything but cartoons." He did try mashing it down like a little kid would and that worked well enough to eat.

They sat in silence for a while as they ate the monstrous sandwiches. Cassandra pulled two bottles of water out of the fridge and downed one quickly. "Need to stay hydrated."

James chuckled and drank from the other one. "Suppose so. Do you work tomorrow?" He had noticed the clock on the stove said 3:27 and knew it wasn't pm. It had been a while since he had seen that small of a number, without the sun being high in the sky.

"Hmm no. I don't work on Thursdays and Sundays. Shop's closed on Sundays. Hate having split days off but Yvette's at a buyer's convention. She's been gone for the last month checking out different lines and display shows. She says it's time to remodel."

"Well, after we wake up in the morning, you'll have to take me. That way I can see it before and after."

"Maybe, maybe. Right now I think it's time for a different kind of food."

"Ahhhhhhhh."

"Oh don't panic. We fed our libidos and we fed our stomachs, now it's time to feed our souls." Cassandra took James' hand, led him to the living room, and hit a button on the stereo. A soft haunting melody played as she stepped in to him. It finally dawned on him Cassandra wanted to dance. "I'm not very good."

"It's okay; we can do the high school prom circle."

"Great." As the man sang about going mad while being haunted by his girlfriend's ghost, they danced a second age-old dance.

After a few songs, Cassandra worked up the courage to tell James about the wine. "James? I think I should tell you something."

"What would that be?"

"The wine was spiked so to speak."

"How can wine be spiked? It's alcohol."

"Well, when I made the wine I added an herb to it... an herb good for men's virility."

"Oh really, so that's why I came three times and felt I could go twice more?"

"Yeah, I had made it for my honeymoon." Cassandra's voice faded out as she finished her sentence.

"Hmmm, to be mad or not to be mad?" James knew he couldn't be mad at her after the amazing night they had shared, were still sharing.

Cassandra waited, holding her breath to see what he would say or do. "I think I should thank you, normally I'm a goner till morning after the first time. Good thing I only had one glass or we might never get any sleep." He leaned down and kissed Cassandra wholeheartedly to show his thanks. "I don't know about you, but right now I'm sleepy."

He picked her up and carried her to her second floor oasis. Hoping she was a typical girl when it came to lingerie, he opened her top drawer and pulled out the nightgown that was on top of the almost overflowing pile. Reaching for the belt of her robe, she asked, "How did you know where to find it?"

"Almost all women keep their lingerie in the top drawer. I took a chance that you fell in to the same group." He sucked in his breath as her robe fell open, "I don't think I will ever get over your body." He pulled the nightgown down over her head, lifted her hair out, and let it cascade over her shoulders. James picked her up and laid her in bed, then pulled his t-shirt off and climbed in next to her. As he did, he was hit with such a feeling of déjà vu it scared him. But the fear faded into love, the kind that burns into the soul and won't leave.

CHAPTER FIVE

Hours later, the morning sun shone through the window. Cassandra woke to an almost empty bed. Freyja had joined them during the night and was currently sleeping on the small of Cassandra's back. "Cat, you know I hate it when you sleep there, right?" Knowing that the cat would only snuggle in farther, Cassandra slowly started to roll over on to her side hoping the cat wouldn't take offense and scratch her but just move off her back. Finally, Freyja gave way and let her mistress have use of her back again. Cassandra sat up and realized she smelled food cooking. She jumped up causing the bed to bounce making Freyja hiss and spit.

"Well, Miss Pissy Pants, serves you right. Now I'm going to have a crook in my back from you sleeping on it for gods know how long."

Downstairs James had found Cassandra's fridge. He woke up starving and horny but refused to wake her up just to soothe his libido, so he came down to soothe his other hunger.

He assumed she would wake up soon. They had gotten over seven hours of sleep and he was sure she would be as hungry as he was. When he saw her leaning against the doorframe in her sexy nightgown, he wasn't sure he was going to get to eat. He could feel his cock swell in a matter of seconds.

"Damn woman, you make it hard for a man to get anything done. I'm starving and I'm not sure which hunger I'm going to cave in to first."

"I do...fooooooood. Whatever you are making smells wonderful. Course any food I don't have to cook is wonderful...I for one hate cooking ; it's such a pain."

"It's just omelets with cheese, bacon and some of the left over sausages I found in your fridge. I hope you don't mind I'm not too much in to veggies before lunch. My omelets are always carnivore specials."

"No, that's fine with me. Don't tell my aunts, but I never outgrew the hate of veggies. I like very few of them."

"I won't tell, if you won't tell."

"Yeah, then they would be over here every day and I would never get a day off. They always want to go to the shop and buy something for some friend or someone. They seem to think they can't go into the store without me, like they're trespassing if I'm not there."

"If you don't want to go in today, that's fine. I can see it another time. I'm sure we can find something else to do."

"Oh no, it's fine. Hopefully we are getting a shipment in with a sweater I have to pick up for Aunt Grace's friend's birthday. I would be going in today no matter what."

"Okay. I just didn't want you to feel pushed into going."

"I'm not. Is that done yet? My hands are starting to shake."

"Shake...are you okay.....why would your hands shake?"

"They're shaking because I've put out too much energy in the last 24 hours and haven't taken in enough rest and food. I'll be okay as soon as I eat."

"Are you sure you're OK? You don't need to see your doctor or something?"

"James, shut up and feed me. I'm fine. It's just because of all the sex and I didn't eat very much yesterday. I was too distracted to eat...the ginseng in the wine didn't help matters either. It's an herb that helps speed up metabolism. So the sandwiches we ate are gone and it was the only meal I've had in about 18 hours. That's all, I promise. I'm fine, just hungry."

"Okay, okay it's ready." She was already sitting at the table. She did look a little pale and not quite steady, even while sitting. He would worry but would wait until she ate to see if she looked better.

"Oh man, those were wonderful...I can never make omelets, I always end up with scrambled eggs with stuff in them."

Laughing, he answered, "It's not hard; it just takes practice. I worked my high school summers as a short order cook at an IHOP knock off. Ya know, one of those breakfast 24 hours a day kind of places, so I had to learn."

"Well you're good." Cassandra looked over at the clock and saw that it was almost one.

"Oh man, it's been a long time since I've slept till one. I suppose if we are going to do anything today we should get moving. Do you want to stop at your place and change?"

"Yeah and shave, I have some wicked 5 o'clock shadow going on."

"Honey, you are so past 5 o'clock shadow it's pathetic. You're well into next day stubble."

"Sorry. Am I that scruffy?"

Cassandra reached over the table and roughed up his chin and said "Sure, but I don't care."

"Well I do, it itches."

"Okay lemme run upstairs and do the girl stuff. I won't be long."

James was certain Cassandra would be a while so he decided to start the breakfast dishes; but fifteen minutes later, Cassandra grabbed his ass and he grabbed his chest.

"Shit woman, don't do that!" he yelped.

"Don't do what? What are you doing?"

"The dishes - I figured I could get them done while you're getting ready. Did you forget something down here?"

"No I'm done. Come on, just throw them in the dishwasher."

"What do you mean you're done? You were only gone ten minutes."

"Fifteen but who's counting?"

"Wait - you got dressed, did your hair in".....he leaned so he could see what she had done with her hair "a real French braid, put on makeup, and you're ready to go, how? No woman ever is ready in fifteen minutes."

"Why not? I prefer to sleep than to get up and spend hours looking in the mirror. It's why I still like myself. I don't look at myself unless I have to. Then I can't find anything wrong with how I look."

"Well that works, I guess. Kind of a guy way of thinking, but that's not a bad thing."

"Nope. You ready? I just have to put my shoes on."

James watched her sashay, 'Yeah, he thought, 'sashay is the right word' into the living room. His cock twitched in his jeans, and he wondered if he could wait until later but the air stirred just right and he caught a whiff of her scent, all of her scents, and that became a very big "no".

He walked into the living room and she as at the coat closet looking for a specific pair of shoes, he guessed.

She was wearing all white; a white not-quite-mini skirt, a white silk tank top and a white knee length long sleeved sweater.

She must have found the shoes she was looking for because she bent down and reached into the back of the closet; her ass was so seductively calling to him. Any fight he might have had in him not to make love to her again was long gone. He took one big step and brushed heavily up against her ass, leaning over her, kissing her ear, breathing softly into it.

"James" Cassandra said softly "I think we need the couch."

He picked her up and gently set her over the back of the couch then he jumped over the back and landed in front of her startling her and making her shout out in surprise.

"Sorry, did..." James stopped short as Cassandra reached for his jean's zipper and pulled it down. James pulled away from her and did the rest himself, he was not going to let her undress him this time.

Cassandra watched James undress in less than ten seconds, a record she was not sure could be beat without basketball tear-away pants.

James knelt down and kissed Cassandra with heavy desire. She returned the kiss with equal yearning. James slid his hand under her skirt to her thigh, rubbing gently as she shuddered. He moved higher up on her thigh and felt the satin of her panties. He pulled her into his lap so that she was straddling him, and he caressed her clit through her panties using the material's texture to drive her wild. She was kissing his neck and sucking on his ears but never staying in one place for long.

James pulled her panties down while lifting her up. He slid two fingers in and used his thumb to play with her clit more. She was making her wonderful mewing sounds again, the sound that turned him to melted butter; she had a small orgasm compared to what she had last night... or was it this morning? He knew she would come again soon.

He slid his fingers out and his cock in. "Oh my god she feels good."

Cassandra was on wave after wave of ecstasy. She couldn't manage a coherent thought, let alone two or three; she was just feeling. She cried out when she came and then again. When she felt him enter her, James just fit.

Cassandra rode James for a long time before he started to feel the tingle.

When he did, it was all at once. He had no time to prepare and shouted out when he finished.

CHAPTER SIX

They leaned against one another for a while but then Cassandra got a Charlie-horse in her calf. "Ohhhhh ow ow ow ow ow ow."

"What, what?" Cassandra moved off James as best as she could and tried to massage the back of her leg, when James realized what was wrong he said "Lie down and I'll rub it out."

Cassandra did her best to lie down without crumbling in to a heap on the floor. James helped her down and began rubbing her leg. "I guess I need to pick up some bananas while we are out. And we might need to clean up again."

Cassandra stopped to think if there was something else, she could use to help raise her potassium levels to stave off any other muscle cramps.

"Sorry - couldn't resist. You smelled so good, just so sexy, and well..." He reached over and rubbed her ass with one hand while still rubbing her cramped calf muscle. She tried to swat at his hand, but it only pulled the knot in her leg making her whimper again. James took pity on her, stopped fondling her ass, and worked on her leg. After a while, the muscle loosened up.

Cassandra was able to stand without wincing too much.

James said "Walking will help work out the rest...I'll help you up the stairs though, just in case."

"Thanks, I don't get them often, thank the gods, but I do get them really bad when I finally get one." Cassandra limped her way to the stairs and sighed at the bottom step. "Well there goes the shoe I was going to wear."

James took her elbow so if she wanted or needed to, she could shift her weight to him. "Okay, I'll bite. What does a leg cramp have to do with shoes?"

"I was going to wear my strapped stiletto heels, but with my calf cramping like that, I better not."

"Well, yeah, I suppose heels wouldn't be smart. Do you have a pair of flats or something short?"

"Yeah, I do. I just wanted to wear those heels. I think I'll be okay now," she said when they got to the top of the stairs. In the bathroom, she closed the door and began to clean up.

James went into the other bathroom and cleaned up. He decided he would bring over a few things: razor, shaving cream, aftershave, deodorant, a few clothes.

Then he realized that he didn't own anything that he cared if he kept. A few CDs, movies, books, some work stuff, but no furnishings or anything like that. He had always passed on taking anything that might mean something somewhere down the road. His sisters had gotten all of the heirlooms because he had told everyone he didn't want them, but here Cassandra had heirloom furniture from her family. He had a sizeable house as part of his salary at the ranch; she had mentioned she had thought about finding another place to live but didn't want to look. He had spent so many nights at Beth's place, never taking more than he needed for that night and the next day. He had never even thought about a future with Beth or any of the other women he had dated. With Cassandra though, he was thinking of a forever future with her and he had only known her one night. He honestly couldn't think of her not being there. She was part of him now.

Cassandra had just finished cleaning up and fixing her hair from their latest sex-capade. She really loved that she could smell James' scent all over her and all over her house. She loved that her skin was slightly raw from his stubbly chin.

CHAPTER SEVEN

They met downstairs where Cassandra opted for the white flats instead of the stiletto heels, and they made their way to her car. "So where to, boss man?"

"Highway 101 for a while. I'll let you know where to turn because the road is hard to find."

"Okay, no problem." Cassandra looked around the sky trying to find any clouds but found none. "Mind if we bring Odin along? He hasn't been on a ride in ages."

"No, that's fine, he can run around the paddock for a while since he is a horse." James tried to get out of Cassandra's reach when she reached over to hit him, but he wasn't fast enough. "Hey, hey, hey! I was kidding. Sort of. Oww! That hurt." Rubbing his left arm where she had hit him.

Cassandra reached in and turned the key enough so she could put the top down.

"Odin's so big that in order for him to G-O I have put the top down, so he can only G-O on nice days."

Cassandra had to spell "go" because if Odin heard the word with his name he would bark like crazy and scratch the door until she got it open. Plus if the convertible top wasn't already down he would try to get in and rip it. Something he'd done before. When she opened the door, he was sitting on the couch, a place he knew he was not supposed to be but one she knew he used daily when she was at work. Something about large amounts of dog hair on a no-dog couch gave him away. "Odin, GO!" She stood back from the door knowing full well that if she didn't she would be sidewalk fodder.

"James, quick, get in or you're riding in the back."

James had made it into the front seat just before Odin got there, and Odin was currently giving James the "eat shit" look that he had perfected on the cat. Cassandra knew the look would fade as soon as they got out of her maze of a parking lot.

James kept thinking about his house and wondering if he should mention his idea. Instead, he decided to wait to see how she reacted to the house. About half an hour later, he told her how to find the back entrance of the ranch. Ten minutes more and he gave her the directions of how to get to the ranch house. The reaction he saw when she pulled up in front of the house was amazing.

"I can't believe you live here. This house is gorgeous. Everything looks so perfect. The lighting here is great. It's bright and open but you still have privacy and I bet the sunsets here are just wonderful. The wood is great too, such nice rich, warm tones. The furniture is a little blah. Well the house is great. Oh sorry, I'm babbling." She turned towards one of the windows and watched Odin run around the fenced yard. He was sniffing everything, peeing on everything, and barking at everything. The drawback to apartment living and having a large dog is they get the short end of the stick.

"He looks very happy out there. He would have a field day when they get the main fence up. This fence is there to keep the broncos that break loose from trampling the trees and stuff. They have trampled this area twice, so Linda insisted that Boss put in a fence to keep her hard work from being destroyed." James shook his head remembering how angry Linda had been the first time it had happened, let alone the second time. "That and the insurance company likes it better this way. They didn't appreciate replacing the top and the door on my jeep because one of the new broncos got loose and kicked them in. This way most everything is safe." James had never cared about the fence before; now it was another reason for her to move in here with him... and bring her exquisite bedroom furniture.

"There're even stairs for Freyja to pounce on us from. She can get Odin from everywhere. Can I see the upstairs?"

"Yeah, come on up. It's gonna be a few anyway. I want to shower and shave, so look around. There are a couple of beers and some juice in the fridge. Glasses are in the cupboard next to it. See you in a few." James disappeared into the last door on the right, so she assumed that was the bathroom.

Cassandra walked into the room at the top of the staircase and saw a beautiful field of some sort of grain through the window. The room was nice but the office furniture really needed to be replaced. It seemed like that James didn't have any belongings that someone would want to keep.

She could easily see herself living in this house for a long time. The animals would love it, and there were two extra bedrooms. When they had pulled up, Cassandra had seen a shop to the side of the house. She wondered what was in it. She would like to have a place to do some woodworking. '*I have too many hobbies,*' Cassandra thought to herself. She liked variety; it was much more fun than doing the same thing all the time. Cassandra had managed to wander her way through all the upstairs and was working on the downstairs. In her mind, she kept redecorating his house with her things; her bookshelf there, her end table here, a plant in that window. She found the fridge and admired the stainless steel behemoth, then was amazed at what wasn't in it. The man did not stock up. It was a fridge that belonged to some cliché movie bachelor. There was cheese, beer, something fuzzy in what resembled a bread wrapper, and a fruit juice she wasn't brave enough to try. She opted for the safety of the beer.

Cassandra peeked in the freezer and there was steak, steak, steak and a chicken. No problems with his taste in food though. The stove was another mass of stainless steel. Four burners with the indoor grill in the middle and what looked like a double oven and a warming drawer as well. Out back she found a wraparound porch, half of it enclosed. There was some very nice deck furniture that somehow she knew came with the house and was not James'. It was just too modern and sleek looking for him.

She stepped out into the yard and whistled for Odin. Within seconds, he was racing around the corner of the house towards her. "DOWN!" she commanded before he even had time to do what was in his dog brain. "Sit," she said more gently. She tipped the beer bottle and gave Odin a small amount.

"Just what the hell are you doing?" She turned towards the strange but familiar voice to see Mark's cousin, Josh.

"Oh my gods!" Cassandra shouted with glee looking at her old friend.

Josh broke into a huge smile. "Still getting your dog drunk I see?"

"Well, are you going to tell Odin no? I don't think so, mister."

Josh was inside the fence by the time she finished her sentence and walked over to Cassandra to hug her.

Leaning back so he could see her, Josh asked, "Heya, cuz, how are you?"

"I'm good, better than I have been in a long time."

"Good, I'm glad to hear it. What the hell you doing out here?"

"James brought me out. He wanted to change before I showed him the shop.

"Change? He's not training today, and your shop isn't that fancy... Never mind." Suddenly getting why James would need to change, Josh then asked, "Should I take him out back and give him the 'If you hurt her' speech?"

"Nope...I'm fine. Thanks for the offer though. How's your aunt?"

"Getting on, she's dealt with it. Uncle Phil is still pretty busted up about Mark's death. He's starting to get a handle on it. Guess you have to, I'm glad. I know how much you two meant to each other. Aunt Janice would still like to see you, you know."

"I know. I have driven over there so many times, but I'd get to the end of the street and wouldn't be able to breathe. I think I will go over soon and see them. I think I might even be able to make it into the driveway now."

"Good, good," Josh gave Cassandra a hug just as James came out the back door.

"Hey now partner, you better not have designs on my girl. I just found her."

"Ha! I found her first buster. I've known her for years. So there."

"What do you mean you've known her for years? She only just got here a little while ago."

"You need to get off the ranch more often. This is not the only place to meet people. This is my cousin's fiancée. Well, ex-fiancée."

"You're Mark's cousin? Sorry man, didn't know."

"That's ok, no big. I was working at the other stead when he died; you and I hadn't met yet. And it's not something people talk about much."

"No, I don't suppose it is. Still…"

Josh shook his head and said, "Man you're bringing down our girl. Get her out of here and show her a good time, would ya?"

"Don't have to ask me twice. If I stick around here, Boss might find something else for me to do. Not having any of that today."

"Good, now git."

"Later, Josh, tell your aunt I'll be over soon."

"Can do," Josh said as he leaped back over the fence.

CHAPTER EIGHT

"I didn't think you would know anyone out here."

"That's OK. I thought Josh was still working over in Clark, but I haven't talked to his family in a long time. It just hurt too much."

"Josh has been over here for about five months, I think. He does good work.

He's helped me several times with the horses. I keep trying to get Boss to let me train him, but he says he needs him as a field manager."

"Josh just likes the outdoors. He doesn't really care what he does so long as it's outside."

"So are we ready to head to the store?"

"I'm ready."

"Let's go then."

James and Cassandra walked to the front of the house where they couldn't see Josh standing in the shade of one of the trees along the corral. He had always liked Cassandra, always thought she was good for his cousin... a man so much more like a brother to him, unlike his own. Losing Mark had hurt him as much as it had hurt Cassandra. He was glad that she had found someone new and that he knew James to be a good man. Josh had felt odd about not being attracted to Cassandra, but the cards just hadn't been played right for that attraction. What most of the guys around here didn't know was that Josh was more likely to make a pass at one of them than their wives. The only one who did know was the boss's wife. She had walked up behind him while he was on the phone with his boyfriend at the time. Janice, like Mark, hadn't judged him. Mark had never gone all funny on him when he talked about his partners or when they hugged or touched. God, he missed Mark! Josh really hoped that everything would work out for James and Cassandra because if it did, then he could dream about being able to find it for himself.

"Oh hey, I don't think so missy." James said as she walked towards her car.

"What? I thought we were going to the shop."

"We are, but I'm driving. We're taking my Jeep because I want to see your hair all windblown and wild. Would you mind taking the braid out?"

"Oh, OK, sure." Cassandra walked over to James' Jeep. She knew that it was a CJ-7 because Mark kept talking about getting one; he had wanted to get into rock crawling and four wheeling. She had always joked that if you wanted to go rock crawling you should do it on your own two feet so that you didn't have to worry about something breaking or rolling over on you.

Cassandra climbed into the blue Jeep, slightly apprehensive about getting into a vehicle with so little to it; it just seemed like it shouldn't be safe. Truthfully, she had only started to worry about things like that since Mark's accident.

James turned up the stereo and backed out of the drive so fast that Cassandra gasped in surprise. James had the canvas soft top on the Jeep because of the heat. There was very little for Cassandra to hold onto, so she grabbed the side of her seat by the door. She didn't want James to see that she was afraid. She knew it was dumb, but he looked so happy and free she didn't want to interrupt him. She decided she would just try to work past her fears and apprehension. Cassandra figured this was just a lesson Freya wanted her to work on - letting go of fears.

Cassandra was right; James was in a moment. He had a girl inches away who he was pretty sure he loved and who loved him, he was in his dream ride, with exactly what he wanted on it, in it, around it, and he had his other favorite girl coming through the speakers of his stereo system. God Bless Gwen Stefani. What more could a guy ask for? He stole small glances towards Cassandra while trying to concentrate on the road.

Jeeps were not made for screaming down a winding highway at 75 mph, but James wasn't looking at the speedometer. He was too lost in his thoughts of Cassandra and their future. He didn't notice when he looked at her that she was becoming more and more pale, while her eyes were getting bigger and bigger.

At the city limits, James slowed down to merge with the flow of traffic. At a stop light, he turned to Cassandra to ask her directions to the shop. "Fuck!"

Cassandra had been in her own little world to retreat from the fear she had been feeling for the last twenty minutes. Hearing James curse brought her back to reality. She slowly turned to James after she shook her head to clear some of the discomfort away. "What?"

"Why didn't you say something?" James yelled, not angry with Cassandra but at himself for not realizing his driving might scare her. It had only been months since she lost her lover to a car accident and here he was driving like a fucking maniac. Damn he was an asshole. He didn't even notice that her color had been draining while he was stealing glances at her. Hadn't even noticed...what a great caring compassionate wonderful guy he was. NOT!

"You," Cassandra's voice squeaked and sounded horse at the same time "you were having fun, enjoying yourself. I didn't want to interrupt you."

His stomach turned itself into a knot and a million butterflies started to fly around as he watched her try to clear her throat. She wouldn't look at him; she was staring out the windshield with a blank look on her face.

The light had changed to green; James hadn't seen it, and drivers behind him were getting upset. Road rage being what it is, James knew it would not be wise to piss anyone off. He shoved the Jeep into first and pulled into the first parking lot he could find.

"Damn it, you should have fucking said something. Damn it, I should have realized it. Fuck! God baby, I'm so sorry." He pulled Cassandra to him and held her. It only made him angrier that she was cold, clammy, and shaking - just a little, but she was still shaking. "Fuck." He said again to himself.

"It's okay. I'm all right. It's not your fault. I just, just, just...I just, I don't know... I just panicked because, well, just a lot of things. This just doesn't seem like it would hold up to much, and you were driving so fast, and seeing Josh started me thinking about Mark, and..."

"It's okay; it is my fault because I didn't think. I'm sorry."

"No it shouldn't have bothered me like this. I should know it doesn't matter what kind of vehicle you're in; they are all vulnerable."

"What do you mean?" James knew his Jeep was not the top for auto crashes but it was pretty damn safe.

"Mark worked for the city and he was in a big Ford Super Duty truck. You know the huge, what do they call them... Quad-Cabs...the kind you can fit like 6 guys in?"

"Yeah I know the one; we have several on the ranch."

"That's what he was driving when he was hit. He was crossing State at that light and this drunk driver ran the light at 65 and hit him dead center in the driver's door. The EMTs said that he was dead before the truck stopped moving. They had to look for parts of his engine everywhere because the drunk's car hit him so hard that it sheered bolts and shattered mounts. They said that Mark's air bags did him no good because of the bad angle and the speed. The driver broke both his legs and his left arm, I think. He fared better because he was drunk and because he was in a much older truck...one that was still more steel than tin or fiberglass. He pled guilty, didn't fight the charges, and made it much easier on Mark's family. I'm not sure Mark's dad would have done too well with a long trial."

"Oh God, honey." She had started to get some color back in her face but now she looked pale again. She had finally stopped shaking though. "Cassandra, I'm sorry, sweetie. God, I'm an idiot."

Cassandra sniffed and sat up pulling away from James. "No, it's my fears not yours. I wanted to try to work past them. I know that Freya brought you to me to work past some things, to move on from what happened to Mark, and this is part of it. I like to drive fast and feel the wind in my hair. But that's just it - I drive. This is one of the few times that I wasn't the one driving. Mark used to always let me drive because that's all he did for the city. So by the time he was off work he didn't want to be behind the wheel anymore. I just am not used to other people driving."

"Ahh I see. So it's a little bit you, a little bit the accident, a little bit me."

"Well, yeah, basically." She gave James a hug and tried to shake off the rest of the uneasiness. "So was this our first fight?"

"Hmm, guess so. Can say I hope it's our last but I doubt it."

"Me too." Cassandra flipped the sun visor down to check her makeup and found nothing.

"Ummm."

"Yeah, this is a guy truck not a chick's...no mirrors."

"Men...." She picked up her purse and took out a compact "You can walk out the door, never check to see how you look until you get home again...it's just not fair."

James just laughed at her, "Sorry - price you paid for eating the apple."

"Ha!...What a load of shit...that's the worst story ever. Don't even get me started on that."

"Oops! Yeah, wrong analogy with the wrong woman."

"Yes sir, it is. Damn, I look like shit... stupid mascara...it's never waterproof, I don't know why they even bother to advertise it. Bunch of liars."

"Look, while you're doing the girl thing why don't you tell me how to get to the shop so we can kill two birds with one stone?"

"Down Market, left at Lincoln, down four blocks to 3rd and down six more blocks to the shop. It's on the left from this way."

"Well hell, that's direct....not. Damn construction."

"That is the easy way to avoid the construction, otherwise I'd just tell you to go down Market to 3rd and back one block."

James shook his head pulling out of the stall; thank the gods or whatever that she didn't look like a damn sheet anymore. He was still pissed at himself for being so thoughtless. Josh would kick his ass for a week when he found out, and he would take it like a man because he deserved it.

CHAPTER NINE

He drove the way she had told him, but it took a lot longer than it should have because everyone was taking the same sub roads to get to the shopping district, as the natives referred to it. It was a large section of town that was higher end shops and small cafés. If Yvette's shop was in that part of town, she was doing quite well. The rent in that part of the district where she was would indeed be high. James spotted the sign for Magical Ways and found a place about four over from the door. It was rare to find any stalls let alone one near where you actually wanted to go.

"Hey babe, we're here. Hell, don't do that to a man, you're bound to kill him."

"What now?" Cassandra asked perplexed...the man was so damn confusing.

"Remind me never to take you to an intensive care unit, please. You'll kill every man and gay woman in the place so long as they can open their eyes."

"What the hell are you talking about?"

"You look like a damn angel, I've thought so since the first time I saw you.

Every time you talked last night I kept picturing angels…angels in leather a few times, but still angels."

"Ummm… thanks, I think."

"I know angels are a Christian thing, but damn it, you do look like one."

"OK. You aren't going to pass out on me are you?"

"Nope, I'm good. I'd just been paying attention to traffic and not you. Last time I looked at you, you looked like death warmed over, so to speak."

"Yuck! Thanks."

"Sorry. Could have said that a little better maybe."

"Yeah maybe. Anyway, since we are here, we should go in. Maybe I should warn you about Melissa."

"Melissa?"

"Yeah, well, Melissa is a little over protective. She, well, she's had an odd childhood. Her mom took off when she was six. Best she can remember her mom had cancer and just couldn't handle having her family watch her die, she left them. So from about six to fifteen it was her and her dad. Her dad loved her and was devoted to her. But one day when she was fifteen, he didn't come home from work. She found out from her dad's boss that her dad's boss was…well, a boss."

"What do you mean a boss? Like what, a mob boss?" James laughed thinking he had to be totally off base.

"Um, yeah actually, she found out at fifteen that her dad was an enforcer for the mob -the guys that go around making people pay up. He didn't do the breaking, I guess he just did the threats...the guy who did the breaking, well he got a better offer from somewhere else and to get the job I understand that he had to ...."

"Okay I get it, 'rub the guy out' as they used to say."

"Yep. Aniello made sure the guy didn't get to enjoy his better offer for long though. This is all through Melissa; you understand I don't know any of these people. But when her dad died, Aniello took her in and made sure she never wanted for anything material. Melissa was afraid of what would happen when she got older, if they would ask her to 'join the family' or something. When she turned eighteen, she told Aniello that even though she knew some of the people she didn't know any of what they had done. And if she promised to never name any who's, she wanted to leave and have a normal life before she found out any what's. And it seemed that he had a soft spot for Melissa 'cause he said that he never wanted their life for her, gave her about forty grand and moved her here; said that if she ever needed anything, legit or not, to call and he would be here as soon as the jet could land."

"Must be nice to know you have that kind of support if needed."

"It would be but she's afraid that there would be strings attached. She tries to stay out of trouble to make sure she never has to call that favor in. She's a little crazy though. She moved here, found the Goth scene, and fit right in. Her hair is never the same color for more than 8 days in a row, she looks like a vampire most days and worries like a mother hen. She's a total mess when Yvette's gone. She was damn near neurotic after Mark died, worrying about me and if I would get too depressed and try to follow Mark. I don't know what I would have done if I had known her when my parents died. I probably would have smothered her in her sleep." Cassandra laughed as an image of purple hair sticking out from under a pillowcase flashed in her mind.

"Okay, so what you're telling me is you work with a more or less neurotic adoptive daughter of a mob boss who worries about everything 'cause she's been left by both her parents, once voluntarily and once not, and to top it off she's a Goth vampire chick."

"Yeah, that's Melissa."

"Okay, that works." He hopped out of the Jeep thinking that his life would never, never, never be boring again. At least he would have great sex with a wonderful woman to look forward too. He opened Cassandra's door and pulled her out of the seat to the street. She lost her balance and leaned against him for support.

"Get a room." Both of them turned to the little old man that walked by shaking his head.

"What was that about?" Cassandra laughed.

"I don't know. It wasn't like I was fondling you or anything." James said as he slid his left hand down to Cassandra's ass, gently squeezing, caressing.

"I know I wasn't doing anything as offensive as groping you in public or anything." Cassandra's hand snaked its way towards James' crotch and what she found was stiff.

"Um, maybe we should get a room."

"Nope, you're going to suffer, just like me. Now come on - we are going in."

"Man, don't say it like that; sounds like we're going into combat or something."

"No, that would be if Yvette was still here and that would only be you. Talk about the third degree."

They walked up to the door. The door was one of the coolest doors he had ever seen. It was covered in ivy frosted onto the glass but instead of the white he was used to, the frosted part looked green and the name was frosted, too, but a metallic purple. "How did you do that?"

"Huh, oh the door? When you first etch something onto glass, if you do it just right, you can add paint to the etching and it will hold the color when you wipe it away. Have to be fast, otherwise the pores in the glass close up, and it doesn't hold."

"Wow, sounds cool."

CHAPTER TEN

As she opened the door, James had a déjà vu moment again because the store looked like her bathroom…there were plants EVERYWHERE! There were probably close to 30 plants in the store, potted ivies ranging in size from small to huge, small palm trees, philodendrons and about ten other kinds he didn't know. "Wow again."

Cassandra laughed, "Yeah, welcome to Jungle East, my bathroom being west. I've taken cuttings from pretty much every plant here and grown them at home. We take turns watering all these guys. It's a little crazy, but we like them."

"I'd say it's crazy." James turned on his heel to see the main section of the store. Clothing was not something he really paid any attention to, but he knew that there was good taste here, good expensive taste. While he was looking around a flash of a moving rainbow caught his attention.

"Cassandra, what are you doing here? You're supposed to be home - you know the whole day off thing."

"I know, I came in to get the sweater set for Aunt Grace's friend. Melissa, this is James."

"Hi." Cassandra had warned James about Melissa but the warning wasn't enough.

"Uh… hi Melissa."

"It's the hair. I know, it's a little overboard, but I just couldn't decide what color this week, so I had Mike do them all. Good thing Yvette's missing this week or I'd be spending extra money on my hair."

"Well it's nice, different."

"Cool." As James's shock wore off he began to notice certain things about Melissa. Her skin was unblemished, but ghostly white and she wore dark blood red lipstick. Her eye shadow, while dark, did not give her that strange raccoon look that he had seen on some of the Goth kids on TV. Melissa's hair was every color in a rainbow, and she was dressed in black from head to toe.

Her shoes were like nothing he had seen in real life apart from on Halloween.

They were boots that came to the bottom of her skirt; they were on six-inch platforms with big silver buckles from ankle to top, which stopped mid thigh.

Her clothes did not come from Magical Ways that was for sure, though it had the look of the same quality. Her shirt was some sort of lace that was see-through with flowing sleeves that had long trailing tips where the cuff would be. Underneath the blouse was a silky looking black tank top that when she moved he could tell it was iridescent and changed shades as the light caught it. The skirt looked like a classic catholic schoolgirl skirt gone dark side. It was short black with several zippers going in various directions and safety pins along the hem.

"Without sounding fashion stupid, what's with the safety pins?"

"Oh, well you never know when you might need one. Be right back."

Melissa grabbed Cassandra's arm and pulled her towards the counter, "Spill it now. Who is he, where did you find him, and does he have a twin brother or sister. I'm not picky."

"Yeah, I know you're not, and he has three sisters, no twins though, sorry, and his name is James. I talked to him last night at the park, and we ended up back at my house and, well..." Cassandra's face started to feel hot and flushed.

Melissa stared at Cassandra, "You didn't, not you. You never do anything like that!" When the realization hit Melissa that Cassandra had slept with someone she just met, Melissa had to bite the insides of her cheeks to keep from laughing.

"Yeah I did. We both had some wine."

"You mean your special wine that you were going to make for your honeymoon with Mark?"

"Well yeah, I made it after he died, I figured I'd just give it as a wedding present at some point."

"But last night you took it out and seduced a man. I couldn't be more proud than if it had been a woman. Oh my God, that's just so me. I'm rubbing off! Damn, where's Emiko? I've got to go corrupt her."

"Oh Mel, will you stop please, just knock it off."

Melissa cringed because she knew Cassandra knew she hated when people called her Mel.

"Hey, she's not in Japan anymore. She needs to learn to survive here; her parents aren't going to find her a nice Japanese old guy to fix her up with if we get her a young hot Japanese guy first."

"Well true, that's kinda weird."

"But we are off topic; topic is you sleeping with an almost stranger."

"Oh gods, make it sound awful why don't you."

"Sex is never awful... well yeah, but no, well you kn...." Melissa trailed off, knowing she was making little sense.

"Yeah I get it."

"So anyway, how was he?"

"Mel."

Failing to hide the smile, Melissa whined, "Oh come on."

"He was good."

"Good or rock your world for the next 5 lives good?" Melissa's face hurt from smiling so big at her friends luck.

"I'll give him 4.5. Don't want him to get a swelled head."

"Yes you do."

"Shut up Mel." Cassandra said watching her friend cringe at the awful nickname.

"I will if you stop calling me that."

"Fine, just go see if Aunt's Grace's stuff is here please?"

"Yep, on it. Go play with the drool-worthy god over there."

"Oh shit, he's found the mannequins."

"Better go explain." Melissa laughed hard as she walked away.

"Yeah."

CHAPTER ELEVEN

Cassandra shook her head as she walked towards James. He had found her mannequin. It was next to Ann's today and, while they were dressed similarly, they looked nothing a like other than their hair color. While Cassandra's was 5'8 and was a petite build, Ann's was only about 5'2 and was heavier set.

They both had brown hair but where Cassandra's had natural red highlights, Ann's was simply brown. Cassandra had often heard Anne lament about getting the short end of all the sticks, but her husband worshipped the ground she walked on so she never changed anything.

Cassandra's look-alike was dressed in a classic box cut skirt with a white turtleneck sweater. Hers looked a lot like Jackie Onassis, while Ann's, dressed in the same skirt with a dark blue sweater, looked nothing like the famous first lady.

"I see you found our Christmas presents from a few years ago."

"Christmas presents?" James asked confused.

"Yeah, Yvette's cousin works in Hollywood on props and stuff, she does life like and life size reproductions of the actors because sometimes they have to die in a bad way. So Yvette asked her a few years ago if she could make mannequins of us. It was fun... well except when she had to do our faces. That part was a pain. Sit there with straws up your nose for about an hour."

"Okay, so who's the other girl?"

"That's Ann."

"How many girls work here?"

"Me, Melissa, Ann, Emiko, and Yvette. The Pagan, the Goth, the Victorian, the Asian, and the Owner."

"The Victorian?"

"Ann likes the Victorian time period. She reads about it all the time.

Dresses more like Queen Ann than Anne Heche though with her body type, Queen Ann is more flattering then Hechte."

"I'll pretend I know what that means."

"Okay."

"Here you go - the present for Grace." Melissa said handing Cassandra a box.

"Thanks. I'll take it over to her in a bit."

"You gonna take him with you?"

"Yeah, why wouldn't I?" Cassandra asked confused.

"Well, because it's your aunt's."

"They're not my parents."

"No, they're worse." Melissa joked.

"Ha ha, not funny."

"She gives me pick-up tips but notice she doesn't share them with you." Melissa pointed out.

"Fat lot you know, she gives me tips all the time, I just choose to ignore them."

"Oh my God." Melissa walked away laughing and was intercepted by a little blue haired lady carrying a tin box.

"What's that about?" James said pointing to the box in Melissa's hand.

"Oh the little blue hairs think Melissa is too thin and so they bring her fattening stuff all the time to try and 'get some meat on her bones' as they say. They try to get her to come with them to bird watch. Stuff out in the park to get her a little bit of a tan, too. What they don't realize is she happens to have that metabolism that all women would kill to possess and that no matter how much time she spends in the sun she never tans, just burns. We keep trying to tell them, but they feel sorry for her, and they all kind of adopt her as this little wayward waif who needs looking after."

It was James turn to laugh, "Yeah, the mob boss's niece needs looking after."

"Niece? I never said that."

"I know but she probably thinks of him like an uncle after he took care of her when her dad died, so it seemed to fit."

"Yeah, I guess she has called him Uncle Aniello a couple of times."

"See? So I want to see the rest of the mannequins"

"All right, I'll give you the grand tour." The first mannequin they came to after hers and Ann's was Emiko's, and James being a guy stated the obvious.

"I bet this is Emiko huh?"

"Yep, what gave you that idea?"

"The eyes."

"Yeah, they are really soft. She is so shy and submissive. She had an arranged marriage set up in Japan."

"They still do that?"

"It's not common practice but yeah. Anyway, her fiancée left her like two weeks before the wedding for a French woman, and her parents held it against her for not keeping him happy. They sent her to live with family here in The States as a kind of punishment. Only the family wasn't doing as well as her parents thought, so she had to get a job to stay. A cousin works at one of the coffee shops down the way and told Emiko that Yvette was hiring. When she came in the first time, she was so scared that she would do something and dishonor her family more. We have started getting her some semi-American ideas. She's not quite so much the lone leaf in the middle of a tornado anymore."

"Well that's good."

"Yeah she wears make up and American styled clothes. Yvette really helped her out; found her an apartment with a couple other Japanese girls that were acceptable to her parents. The family she had been staying with here ended up moving back to Japan and living with family there so that was pretty easy."

"I can imagine if they are mad enough to send her away they aren't going to want her back any time soon."

"No they don't. So Melissa has taken it upon herself to find her a good man, one that is way better than the guy her parents had picked for her. That way they will have them eating crow for the rest of this life time and some of the next."

"Hmmm, she's got a good heart."

"Yeah, she takes Emiko to good places to find handsome, young, successful, Asian guys and tries to get her to talk to them." Cassandra explained.

"If she's that shy I bet that doesn't work too well."

"No it doesn't. She did say 'hi' to the last guy, so there is progress."

"Cool." James looked at the small, demure, mannequin, and felt a stirring in his heart. He couldn't understand anyone sending a shy girl away to a world unknown to her, to a family she didn't know. The big brother urge to pound the hell out of someone who had hurt his sisters was growing. Emiko was maybe 5'4 and just as thin as Melissa. The artist who had cast and painted her face was so good. He kept waiting for it to blink. Her eyes were the traditional brown, but they had jade green flecks. Her hair was onyx black, silky, shiny, and stick straight. He turned away from the sad face before he gave in to the urge to beat something bloody.

"What?" Cassandra asked James.

Caught off guard he didn't know what Cassandra was asking, "Huh?"

"You look so mad, like you're about to kill something." Cassandra didn't add that she could literally feel the anger rolling off of him.

"I am pissed. Man, if anyone had treated any one of my sisters that way, he would have permanently become a soprano. If he survived at all, not only because I would have pounded him, but the other two sisters would have stepped in.

"You're feeling what we all felt when we first found out. I had forgotten how pissed we were when she first told us, but I've had two years to get over it and watch her blossom into a more secure and independent girl. She doesn't call home every other day now, only once a week. She has her own friends besides us, and she is less shy, well, at least around people she knows."

Cassandra took a deep breath and pulled up her shields a little tighter. James' anger was stinging her like a thousand needles.

"You're not making it better, love."

"It really is better. She goes out, trust me, that's a LOT better."

"All right, come on and show me the rest."

CHAPTER TWELVE

Cassandra showed James the rest of the store and Melissa and Yvette's mannequins. Melissa he only recognized because of the pale skin color and the bright blue eyes.

"No way that's Melissa, her hair is blond."

"Yeah I know, but that's what color her hair really is."

"California Sunshine surfer girl blond."

"Yep."

"How?"

"She's from California."

"I thought mob stuff was all back east, New York and stuff."

"Guess not."

"Well you learn something new every day. So if that's Melissa, that must be Yvette."

"Yep, that is our fearless leader, Yvette Lacroix." Cassandra said.

"Lacroix."

"Yeah, she's Cajun," Cassandra answered, laughing.

"With a name like that she better be."

"That's why she so understands about paganism," Cassandra mentioned, "Half her family is

Voodoo priests. Well, not quite that many, but a lot. They are all in Louisiana."

"How many were messed up because of the hurricane?"

"A few lost homes and shops, but they all got out okay. They are rebuilding now. It's one of the reasons Yvette's been gone for so long."

"Going back and checking on them all?"

"Yeah, kind of."

"She looks like a mother hen."

"That title suits her to a 'T'. She and Melissa can smother a person to death."

"I bet." James shook his head. All the girls here were so slender except Ann, but she looked good even if she was a bit heavy.

Yvette looked like she spent all her time in the sun; her skin was a warm bronze tan that looked slightly olive, as if she had Mediterranean heritage.

Her hair was a dark and rich mahogany like Cassandra's, but seemed even darker, like the wood had aged hundreds of years. Her eyes were not the bright clear blue of Cassandra's but a dark and stormy blue. He'd seen that color of blue in the sky a few times before. It was always before a bad flash floods or rainstorms on the desert when he worked as a hand. It was an eerie foreboding color, which no ranch hand ever wanted to see while in open country.

"It's her eyes, huh?"

"Yeah, they're that…"

"That scary blue."

"Yeah, I've seen that blue in nature a couple of times. It's not a good color to see when you're out in the open range."

"I can imagine."

"That's the shade the sky is before nasty thunder and rain storms that tend to bring flash floods."

"Have you ever been caught in one?"

"No, I made it to shelter before the two that could have caught me, and I was far enough away from the third that it was spooky to watch from start to finish without having to look over your shoulder while trying to get the hell out of there."

"I love the storms, the energy they give off, the sheer excitement."

"I get to watch some good ones at my place."

"I bet that deck is a great place to see them, curl up on the swing with a wool blanket and a hot cup of something good, and just watch the mother go to work."

"I usually choose a beer and fleece but yeah, same concept."

CHAPTER THIRTEEN

Both Cassandra and James were lost a little bit in the thought of sharing a storm together that they didn't hear Yvette walk out of the storage room towards them. In her unique Cajun/New York accent she drawled, "You know it's not polite to stare at someone's likeness. Some people think you're trying to steal the soul to control it."

The two daydreamers jumped simultaneously.

"Yvette! Oh my gods. You're supposed to be gone."

"Yeah, going to leave Thursday instead to see Moira."

"Oh, has she had the babies yet?"

Yvette shook her head with exasperation, "No, the woman is being the most obstinate mother. She says she's not having the babies until they decide it's time to be had."

"Why can't Donovan talk some sense into her?"

Yvette shook her head, her auburn hair swishing behind her. "Because he's just so worried about her. His usual persuasive personality has gone right out the window when we need it the most. The doctor is threatening her with a court order."

"Oh gods, they are a bunch of crazies aren't they?"

"Yeah, they are and I love every one of them."

"I know you do." Cassandra gave Yvette a big hug and a kiss on the cheek.

"So who's this looking totally lost in my store?"

"Oh, this is James."

"Well, welcome, or do you not talk."

"I talk when a woman lets me; I have three sisters, a mother with two sisters of her own and a father with two more. I don't interrupt women when they talk."

"Yep, he's a keeper."

"Yvette, will you stop?"

"Nope, a man who knows his place is a keeper. Is he good in bed? Oh wait, you wouldn't know yet."

"Yeah um, uh, well...anyway..."

"Oh my, Melissa has rubbed off on you hasn't she?"

"I think I missed something."

"No you didn't, it wasn't thrown at you."

"Yvette, stop."

"Fine, chéri, I will for now."

"That's it, I'm out of here. I need to go feed Freyja. Call my cell if you need anything. I most likely won't be home tonight," Cassandra said exasperation coloring her voice.

"Can do, be careful and James?"

James had started to move towards the door but stopped and turned towards Yvette.

"You hurt my chéri and you and I will go around for a very long time and you won't enjoy a single moment of it. There will be no tap outs and no bells to save your pretty Adonis body." And with that hanging in the air she glided off towards a customer looking at one of the outfits that Cassandra's and Ann's mannequins were wearing this week.

"Yep, she's just as scary as the storms."

"Yeah, I would have...um...warned you a little more if I'd known she was here. She really is a big sweetheart. She's just had some bad luck with men and so is over protective of her babies."

"Last I looked you weren't a baby."

"No I'm not, but no one has gotten the nerve to tell momma bear over there. It may look like Yvette could be blown over in a good wind, but she would take the wind in a three count given half a chance."

"I'll say it again - as scary as the thunder storms."

"Come on, let's get home and feed my cat before she tears up my curtains."

"It's not that late, didn't you feed her before we left?"

"I know. Freyja has a very strict diet. It's the 'I eat every 6 hours during daylight or I tear your house to shreds' diet. That's how it goes when you have a psycho kitty."

"And you keep her?"

"Why would I get rid of her?"

"Well if she tears your house apart..."

"Only if I don't do what she likes, so I do what she likes and my house is safe."

"What if you're out of town or something?"

"I take her with me. She travels really well so long as I feed her every six hours. It's not that hard to do really. Besides I like her and she likes me."

"So long as you feed her every six hours."

"Only during the day. I don't have to wake up at night to feed her. I would draw the line there."

"Why don't you just get a bigger bowl and put more food in it, and then she could eat whenever."

"She does have one. She has to have her wet food every six hours. Besides, if I left out wet food for her she would never get it because Odin would eat it all. I tried that once. She lost three pounds before I found out what Odin was doing. The only reason he doesn't eat her dry food is because apparently it tastes awful to him, but she likes it. I haven't found a wet food that works out the same way yet."

"Jeeeez, what a cat."

"Yep, she is."

They walked to James's Jeep and climbed in while James asked Cassandra the best way to get to her apartment from the store.

"To the bridge and then left."

"That works."

CHAPTER FOURTEEN

Cassandra wondered if Aunt Grace would be at the shop she owned with her two sisters, Tabitha and Monica. They all shared a storefront and practiced their varying styles of herbalism. Between the three of them, they covered western, Arvada, Chinese, European, some South American as well as some Native American knowledge of herbs. Cassandra was sure there wasn't anything they couldn't help, cure or make better if they put their minds to it. Cassandra was sure that one day they would figure out a cure for cancer, AIDS, and the common cold all at the same time, and she was also sure it would include garlic in the recipe somewhere.

Cassandra hopped out of the Jeep when they pulled in front of her apartment.

She had gotten mildly used to the Jeep now, though not totally.

Freyja was sitting on the ledge in the front window flicking her tail "Oh crap."

"What?"

"She's doing the rattlesnake thing." Cassandra said hurrying to her door.

"Huh?" James asked, he was confused as to how a cat was like a rattlesnake.

"She has this thing she does when she's pissed off. She flicks her tail like a rattlesnake. That's how she lets you know she's pissed. But it's when she doesn't let you know and is calm that you have to worry 'cause that's when she gets you and you don't know its coming. Psycho kitty."

"Yeah."

Fortunately, Freyja was not mad; she had been watching some crows in the driveway that James had scared away. She had been hoping to get a chance to chase them when Cassandra opened the door.

"Alright, evil, let's get you fed."

"That cat is not evil and you know it," came a voice from behind the couple.

"Aunt Tabitha!"

"That was my name last I checked."

"I was going to head over to the shop in just a few, but needed to feed the demon first."

"I don't know why you put up with this, Freyja. Just come home with me," Tabitha said to the cat in jest, watching the bundle of grey, brown, black, tan and white nibble on the food in her bowl.

"Oh stop. You know she won't go. She likes antagonizing me too much. Me and the dog."

"Speaking of the little king, where is he?"

"He's at James's house."

"James?" Tabitha said her head tilted.

"Me."

Tabitha turned towards the sound of an unfamiliar male voice, to see a man looking very comfortable in her niece's breakfast nook.

"Well, James."

"Aunt Tabitha this is James Austin. James this is Tabitha Winters."

"Ms. Winters."

"I do believe if you had a hat on, you would have tipped it."

"Yes ma'am."

"Is he ..." Tabitha started.

Cassandra said simply, "No," knowing what question her aunt was asking before she finished asking it.

"Oh well, can't have it all." Tabitha replied.

"Yes, I can and often do." Cassandra said trying to sound more confident than she had felt in some time.

"No you don't or you would have been in the..."

"Shut up Tabitha, leave the girl alone," Monica ordered. A mirror copy of Tabitha walked into the kitchen.

"Monica, leave me alone. I really have had..."

"Enough of my nagging, bickering, yes, yes, yes, I know."

"Oh you two really, I can't leave you alone for even a moment. You are going to be the death of me yet. Hello love." Grace leaned over and kissed Cassandra in a kind of European one kiss on each cheek way.

The third copy that had walked in looking the same as the first two, or as much alike as they could look with extremely different styles.

Tabitha it seemed was about an inch taller than Cassandra and roughly the same weight. Her shoulder length wavy hair was a remarkably similar shade of brown to Cassandra's but with a streak of pure white along the left side of her face. She wore tailored clothes that looked of the same style to what the Cassandra and Anna mannequins were wearing in the store.

Monica, the second to walk in, had the same build as Tabitha, but her white streak was on the right side of her mid-back-length, spiral-curled hair. Her clothes and make up looked like a tame version of Melissa's. Her dress, however, was the polar opposite of Melissa's in length. While Melissa had worn a micro mini skirt, Monica's dress almost touched the floor. The shirt looked identical to the one he had seen Melissa in a not long ago, the exception being the undershirt was not the weird iridescent color but a bold burgundy long sleeve shirt.

By a process of elimination, the final aunt to come in would be Grace; she looked like Grace Kelly and appeared to act like her as well. Her clothes were tailored, but with a wistful and flowing style, kind of like an ethereal Glinda, the good witch, without the wand and crown. The subtlety of her makeup made it difficult for James to be sure she even had any on. In addition, the odd white streak ran down the middle of her hair, which was the same shade as that of her sisters and niece, but Grace's hung straight and
was somewhere between Tabitha's shoulder-length and Monica's mid-back-length.

"And here are the other two weirdo's I call family. I've already introduced you to Tabitha. Monica is who Melissa wants to be when she grows up and then we have Aunt Grace who is just, well, Aunt Grace."

"Ladies."

"I was heading over to the shop in a little while. I was bringing you Mary's set."

"Oh thank you, just in time. Her birthday is in a few days." Grace said.

"I know. That's why I was bringing it over. I figured you'd want to wrap it and all."

"Thank you, dear. So who is this?"

"I was just introducing James to Lefty and Righty here." James looked at Cassandra wondering why she would call her aunts that and then it dawned on him - that was which side their odd stripes were on. "James, this is Grace. Aunt Grace, this is James Austin."

Grace extended her hand to James and when he took it, she turned his hand over and began tracing the lines in the palm of his hand. "Good lines, though I'm sure you've looked, dear," Grace said to Cassandra over her shoulder.

"Ah, his life and affection lines are good, strong, and long too. A funny little hiccup in the affection line though, so we will have to watch that. Going to have to change careers soon from the looks of the fate line. We will all be here for you when you struggle with that decision. Both the head and sun lines look well placed, it seems."

"Aunt Grace you're scaring the normal. Can we wait for the past lives till later?"

"I suppose I could put it off for a while," Grace said with a smirk, that didn't seem to fit on that classically beautiful face.

"What was all that about?" James asked Cassandra under his breath.

"Aunt Grace reads palms and other things."

"Other things????"

"Yeah, we'll talk about it later," Cassandra offered with a shrug.

"And the 'normal' remark?"

"Well, the aunt's are all special, talented in certain ways, when it comes to magic. Nothing like in the movies but they are extra," Cassandra said with another shrug. "So as an inside private family joke we tend to call other people normals 'cause, well, we aren't normal."

"Ah."

"Not insulted or upset are you?"

"No, I'll just think about it later."

"Okay."

"So what are your plans for this evening, you two?" Monica asked as Tabitha elbowed her in the side and Grace just shook her head.

"Let the two of them have their time, Monica," Tabitha said, looking offended on James' behalf.

"No, it's fine, I would love to treat you ladies to dinner. It would give us a chance to get to know each other better. All of us." James looked at Cassandra and squeezed her hand.

"It would be fun. And we do all need to talk and learn about each other."

"Okay, it's settled then. Marco's in half an hour." Monica sauntered out of Cassandra's apartment.

"And Goth girl gets her way." Tabitha stalked out but somehow also managed to saunter.

"We will see you soon, dear. Go get ready."

"So do I want to ask what Marco's is?"

"It's a newer organic restaurant that we help out as often as we can."

"Organic? So all chick vegetarian food?" James sounded unimpressed.

Cassandra laughed "No. Yes, they have good salads and vegetarian dishes but they have lots of meat. All of it is free range or grain fed. Its food the way you SHOULD eat it."

"Oh cool, I can go for that. I would have done the chick food, too, but I would have had to stop at McDonald's on the way home."

"Marco would die if anyone had to go somewhere else to fill up after eating at his place. He prides himself on large but healthy portions. He doesn't want people to eat too much and get fat, but he wants everyone to go home satisfied."

"Marco sounds like a guy I could learn to love."

"Most people feel the same way."

"So is it a fancy place? Your aunt said 'get ready'."

"No. It was her way of letting me know if we were late because we get waylaid in the bedroom, it was OK."

"Um, so she was saying it's OK to have sex?" James had a look of terror mixed with awe and amusement all at the same time.

"We all have healthy yet probably abnormal views on sex. It should be had, and as often as possible. If you're a little late for a family function, then you better be smiling and glowing."

"Oh God, what have I got myself into?" James mumbled to himself.

"A really weird family compared to most. But it's a good weird."

"Can I reserve judgment on that till later? Say five or six years from now."

"The fact that you used years as a time frame...yes." Cassandra murmured as she kissed his cheek.

"Thanks, babe," James answered as he did the same thing. "Should we go then, if we don't need to change?"

"Yeah, we can head over...unless you want to take Aunt Grace's invitation?"

"Um, I think I'll wait till after dinner...it would be nice to leave them at the restaurant all night wondering if we are shagging ourselves blind." James asked with a wiggle of his eyebrows.

"James!"

"What? It's your weird family."

CHAPTER FIFTEEN

As mortified as Cassandra was at James' analogy of shagging each other blind, the thought of making love to him again was turning her on. Cassandra stepped closer to James sliding her palms up his chest and asked, "Well, we could try and see if we could maybe cause a little haziness at the very least." "We could, at that." The rest of what he was going to say left his mind as Cassandra kissed him, while unbuckling his belt. When it was unhooked, she worked the zipper of his pants, and slid them down, taking his now rigid cock into her mouth. James luckily was standing close enough to the stairs to lean against the wall, because all muscle control was no longer under his control. Cassandra's mouth did things to his cock that he wasn't sure were legal in this universe. She pulled his sac and gently rolled his balls around while stroking the skin between his balls and his ass. He had heard that was an excellent spot but no one had ever touched that small strip of skin.

Cassandra began alternating between massaging his balls and rubbing his cock but never stopped sucking him. James knew he wouldn't last long and unknowingly began pulling Cassandra's hair, matching her rhythm. Soon Cassandra didn't have to move her head at all. James had completely taken over and was doing all the work. She just kept working his balls and his perinea. When she was sure he was about to come, Cassandra leaned forward and swallowed his cock and slid her finger up towards his ass. Ready or not, James came down the back of her throat yelling her name as he did.

Cassandra was so wet at this point; she was almost dripping through her white panties. James slowly came back to Earth and saw that Cassandra was panting with her own pent up lust. He knew that it was going to be a while before his friend was ready for her again. He laid her down on the floor, pulled her drenched panties off, and slid three fingers in so fast she gasped in surprise. Her eyes quickly glazed over as her orgasm built with lighting fast speed. James figured turn about was fair play, so he began playing with her perineum. If it felt that good to him, it had to feel good for her, too.

Cassandra's orgasm didn't take as long to build as his had, but as she reached hers, he slid his finger down towards her ass and rimmed her little circle. She came so hard she curled into the fetal position to move away from the stimulation, just lying there shivering from the aftershocks. James lay gently next to her and waited 'till she turned to him.

With the most innocent look he could muster, James asked, "Was that good enough to be late for dinner?"

Cassandra just laughed. "Yeah, I think so. I'm going to have to go change and fix my hair, though."

"I'll help."

"Oh no you won't or we won't ever get to dinner."

"Fine," James said in a crushed kind of voice.

"You just get yourself cleaned up," Cassandra said to him.

"Fine," he said again.

"Oh don't whine. You can use my bathroom, you just can't help me."

"Okay."

"Oh God, you're worse than a little kid," Cassandra said smiling.

"Yep, I can be."

They both stood and walked up the stairs to her bathroom, "Ya know, I don't know if I'll ever get used to this bathroom... The plants are just so huge."

"I tell you it's the steam. They just love it."

"The skylight doesn't hurt either." James commented back.

"Well no, but it's the steam."

"If you say so, love."

"I do." Cassandra replied.

"Hmmmmmm, say that again."

"What?" Confused Cassandra asked, "What?"

"I do."

"You want me to say 'I do' again."

"Yep."

"Why?"

"So I can hear it."

"I …Do." Smiling Cassandra drew out the words.

"Hmmmm, one more time."

Cassandra laughed but granted him his simple wish. Truth be, told she had liked saying it and enjoyed him teasing her into saying it just as much.

"Oh God, that's so hot. I don't know if we are going to make it to dinner, you're so damn tempting."

"YES, we are...remind me to never give you ginseng ever again."

"This is not some stupid plant; this is me being incredibly over the moon in lust for you."

"Ha. I see you didn't say love."

"Don't want to say it all the time 'cause then it might not mean something when I do say it."

"Hmmm, sorry, doesn't work that way."

"Well, can't blame a guy for trying can you?"

"I'll think about it."

CHAPTER SIXTEEN

James hugged Cassandra then began washing his face and hands, Cassandra disappeared into her bedroom to change her panties. She briefly thought about changing clothes but decided against it as it would give the Aunts too much to talk about after she and James left. She looked for her lint brush instead and made sure there was no dog or cat hair on her. She took the brush into the bathroom asking James to check where she couldn't reach.

"You're clean, babe. No Odin or Freyja, though that may be a weird thing."

"No, I try to keep their hair down to a dull roar."

"A never-ending losing battle, I would say."

"Well yeah, I did say try."

Ten minutes later, they pulled up in front of a massive three-story mansion.

"I thought you said we were going to a restaurant."

"I did and we are."

"This doesn't look like a restaurant."

"It is, trust me."

When they got almost to the door, it opened. A well-dressed boy of maybe 14 ushered them in and showed them to their table. "Have a nice evening, Ms. St. James."

"You too, Louis."

"He is so big. I can remember when he could barely open that door," Monica said watching the young man walk away.

"I know, he's so cute now too. I bet Marco and Angelina will have their hands full in a few more years."

"A few more? Oh no, Ms. St. James we have them full now."

"Oh Angelina, how is everyone doing?" Cassandra answered the little Italian.

"Good! The baby is in kindergarten and Larissa is in 5th grade now...too big to go to baby school - that's what she calls daycare. Now she comes home and terrorizes us while we try to get things ready each night."

"Maybe you could talk her into it, if she was 'helping' the day care instead of going to the day care. You know, helping get drinks and snacks and that kind of thing."

"We tried that. She's too smart."

"Yes she is." Grace said nodding her head in agreement.

"Who do we have here?" Angelina asked tipping her head in James's direction.

"This is James Austin. James, this is Angelina Costa, Marco's wife."

James nodded to Angelina. He would have stood, but Cassandra had him pinned next to Tabitha.

Angelina's eyes lit up after she looked at James and then at Cassandra.

"He's yes, tell me." Angelina questioned Cassandra hoping that the man's presence there meant that Cassandra had moved on from her lost fiancée.

"Yes, him."

"Oh thank the mother, I'll be right back." She took off like a shot to what James thought was the kitchen. The loud noise that spilled in to the room as the door swung open confirmed his suspicion.

"Will someone please tell me why everyone is so excited when they see me with you? It's not like you joined a convent or something, is it?"

"No, I didn't. Everyone saw how happy I was with Mark after my parents died, and then when he left, too…well everyone was just afraid I might do something."

"Ah-ha, so they are figuring that I'm your stay-out-of-the-loony-bin card."

"Um yeah, I guess so." Cassandra said with a look James wasn't able to decipher.

"OK, just so I know what to expect."

He didn't expect that a giant Italian man would come out of the kitchen straight for their table with tears streaming down his face.

"Marco, what?" Cassandra started to ask but was interrupted by the large man.

"Oh, my little angel, I was so worried that you would be all alone in the world, no one to give you bambinos, no one to give you love on the long winter nights, no one to help you forget the hot summer nights."

"MARCO!!"

"Ah, my Angelina, do not be mad for me. I love this one as if she were one of ours."

"I know you do Marco, and it's mad at you, not for you."

"Ah yes, someday."

"Ah!!" Angelina threw her hands in the air in frustration, spinning on her heels.

Cassandra stood up and hugged Marco, and told the burly Italian everything was fine and that she never feared not having babies, that there were many ways to have babies. He just laughed and told her there was only one good fun way.

At that point, Angelina pulled her husband back towards the kitchen. However before she took him very far he broke from her and pulled James from his seat dragging him to the kitchen. The aunts and Cassandra just watched knowing there was nothing they could do to keep Marco from whatever

mission had
popped into his head regarding James.

"You…"Marco said poking James squarely in the chest with his beefy callused finger. "You…" he said again. "What your plans are for my cara, you better have good ones."

"Um, I'm sorry. I didn't know she was your Cassandra."

"She's mine because I say so. She has no man in her family so I point myself."

"You mean you appoint yourself."

"Yes that is what I said."

"Yes sir."

"So?"

"My plans so far sir, are to make sure that she loves me and trusts me and that when she's ready, to make her my wife. Right now we have known each other for about 24 hours."

"No one knows you, and Cassandra is very fragile. We want to make sure you are good for her."

"MARCO, LEAVE THE MAN ALONE."

"Ma mia moglie che sono. Vedo che le sue intenzioni sono verso il nostro bel Cassandra di angelo. Voglio sapere che è veramente l'un vuole e che la vale."

"I don't care, you soft hearted old man, she is smart enough to know what she wants and has brains enough to know that he is a good man to take care of her." Angelina yelled to Marco while dragging James out of the hot steaming loud kitchen back to the cool dining area and to the St. James table.

"What did he say back there?"

"Just that he was being nice to you and that he was just feeling you out, so to speak, for Cassandra to make sure you were worthy of her."

"Ah, well tell him I am and will try my hardest to continue to be."

"It won't do any good. He is worse than a mother hen when it comes to his 'angels.' He frets and worries over them as if he was an ol' grandmother waiting to see her great grand bambinos so that she could go on to those she's already lost."

"Is that an Italian thing?"

"Yes."

"'Kay, as long as I have that clear."

"Nothing is ever clear, mio caro."

"I'm learning that in a hurry."

"Good, then you are smart enough for her."

CHAPTER

SEVENTEEN

The waiter was standing at the table with menus; he just shook his head when James slid in next to Tabitha. "Marco get to you?"

James shivered when he answered, "Yeah, looks like."

Miguel laughed lightly, "Should have seen him go for Mark when he came in with Cassandra the first time."

"Where is Cassandra?"

"In the ladies room, I'll go get her," Monica offered.

The waiter moved so Monica could get out of the booth but watched her as she walked away. When he finally tore himself from the hall, where she had walked down his face said everything.

"Does she know?" James asked the love-sick waiter.

"Doesn't even know I'm on the same planet."

Tabitha looked at James and said "She's not really into men; she much prefers her partners to have hair as long as hers and have breasts about the same size."

"Ah, didn't know that."

Monica arrived back with Cassandra as Tabitha finished her statement "That's not true I like everyone equal. I just happen to be finding women more to my taste at the moment." James saw the hope jump into Miguel's eyes and watched the man sigh with a desperate prayer, no one else saw because Monica was blocking Miguel from the table.

Monica finally got her skirt under control and slipped into her seat next to Grace. Miguel shook himself and started reciting the specials of the night.

Everyone placed their orders for food and drinks.

"What was with the little boy at the front door, what did you call him, Louis?"

"Oh yes. When he was about nine, he wanted so much to help that they made a job just for him. Marco put in one of those CCV cameras and a TV in the coatroom. When Louis sees people on the TV, he opens the door for them and takes their coats. We figure in a few more months they will let Larissa do that, and let Louis bus tables."

"Larissa is the one that's too smart to go to daycare?" James asked clarifying all the new names.

"Yes."

"Angelina was telling us when Marco had you that Louis has had a couple dates already. And one of them had Marco's mother up in bibles."

Being brave James asked, "Okay, do I dare ask why?"

"It seems young Louis isn't sure which team he's going to bat for yet."

"Meaning he dated a boy and grandma had a stroke?" James asked.

"Yes." Grace nodded.

"Dad didn't?"

"No Marco is a very different kind of fellow." Tabitha added.

"I gathered that."

"Angelina just wants her babies to be happy. Besides her brother is gay, so she's okay with it," Grace supplied.

"Ah."

"He actually hit on Marco the night Angelina and Marco met. Marco said he was never sure if he got the prettier of the two," Monica offered up.

"Yeah and Angelina usually bashes him over the head with whatever is handy," Cassandra said laughing.

"Well yeah, I didn't say it wasn't at great bodily risk." Monica winked.

Miguel returned with their drinks and appetizers. James had ordered the house clam chowder, which was his favorite, New England. The girls had all gone with salads. He just stared at the size of the salads.

"My God, that alone could be a meal." The dinner plates were heaped with a variety of leafy greens. James had known there were different types of lettuce, but he never knew there were so many. "What is in that thing?"

Monica explained, "Five kinds of lettuce, chard, cabbage, carrots, spinach, and many types of herbs."

"Wow."

James watched Miguel...when he set Monica's salad in front of her, he brushed his fingers over the top of her right hand. He also saw Monica raise her hand into his fingers. He really hoped that if they did get together that Miguel's heart wouldn't break more than if he never had a chance with her.

"So James, why don't you tell us about yourself? That is why we all came out to dinner."

"Hmm, well I guess I can hit the highlights and you can ask questions of the stuff that interests you."

"That sounds fine," Grace said eating and James wondered if she did anything ungracefully.

Cassandra leaned over and whispered the word "No." in his ear.

He was startled and looked at her.

"She does everything gracefully because that's who she is. No, I can't read minds, it's just the same question everyone asks."

"Oh. Um, yeah, highlights. Born February 19th 1975, mom and dad are Susan and Jason. I have three younger sisters: Renee, Michelle and Monique. Graduated 1993 wasn't very good at math, so I never tried to get into college. I worked with horses beginning in my junior year of high school and decided that I wanted to keep it up. I've worked on a couple different ranches, but I've been with the Double L the longest. I've worked my way up from mucking stalls to training thoroughbreds."

"What does the double L stand for?"

"Well, I know one of the L's is for the owner's wife, Linda. Everyone thinks the other L is for the boss, but no one knows the boss's name. Or if they do, they are not telling. They don't have any kids that anyone knows about either."

"Ah. What about your family? Are you close?"

"We speak often, though we don't see each other all that much."

"Why not?" Tabitha asked between bites of salad that was more white than green since she had smothered it with ranch dressing.

"Because my sisters all live back east and my parents live in Washington. We get together at

Christmas time at one of my sisters houses because of the kids. Suppose when I have kids I'll be added to the rotation."

"Rotation, huh?"

James couldn't quite decide if Cassandra was mad or not by the look on her face. "This year it is at Monique's house. Last year was Renee's and next year will be at Michelle's. That way no one is screwed with all the extra work of having twenty-some people show up at their house every year. It seems easier this way."

"Why aren't you in the rotation now? What do kids have to do with it?"

"Well 'cause until last year I was in apartments - no room. Kids generally mean house-type living."

"You have a house."

"I know but Monica loves her turn. Her husband lets her repaint when it's her turn. So she doesn't give it up."

"Oh I see. So if you wanted to you could have it here next year?"

"I suppose so, I can see about next year but it's too late for this year. Everyone has already bought plane tickets.

Would you come with me to my family's Christmas this year?" he asked on impulse.

"I suppose I could be talked into it, as I have said I would marry you, so they are my family too."

"What?" the striped ones yelled simultaneously.

Now it was Cassandra's turn to back pedal, stutter and stammer. "Well, um, he, uh asked and I, well, I said..um, well... yes."

Marco came running out having heard the sisters over the loud noise of the kitchen. "What?!" he demanded.

"We are fine Marco. Go - you have a kitchen to run."

"What?" he insisted more calmly this time.

"Okay, you'll know soon enough. James asked Cassandra to marry him and she agreed," Tabitha finally answered him.

"Oh really, wonderful, fantastico, meraviglioso. Champagne for you all!"

"No, Marco no, we are fine honest."

"I insistere."

"Darling, you're speaking in two languages again," Angela said as she walked up to the table.

"Hm, my dolce?"

"You're speaking Italian and English combined again."

"No certo I am not, caro."

"Why do I bother?"

"Because you love him and you are you." Cassandra spoke hoping to change the conversation to something other than the announcement at hand or at least the way the announcement had been made.

"I know, I'll get the bottle."

Marco had started to sing an Italian love song to the newly engaged couple.

"So when were you going to tell us?" asked Grace.

"Tonight. It just hadn't come up yet."

"It is up now. You are not an overly impulsive person, Cassandra."

"I know. I know we haven't known each other long, but we both just knew. "

"Instantly."

"We understand, Cassandra, we do. Your parents were the same way. They dated a while before they got married, but they still knew the first night."

"Cassandra and I will take our time, ma'am. But we knew we loved each other before the night even started."

"We are happy for you both, James. Believe me, we are. We want our 'child' to be happy. Cynthia was our littlest sister and Cassandra is ours as much as she ever was Cynthia's."

James felt he understood what Grace had been saying and returned her smile.

Angela was back with champagne and glasses. Marco took the bottle and like a true show boater, opened the bottle with such flourish he looked as though he was doing a well-choreographed dance. The finale of which was the brilliant stream proceeded by the signature "pop", all the while still singing his Italian song in his beautiful rich baritone voice.

CHAPTER EIGHTEEN

All the customers had turned to watch Marco and were drawn into the scene. What almost everyone could see was Grace as the peaceful leader, who all would follow without question, because they knew she would lead without fail in the right direction. They could see the radiating confidence from Monica, and the pure independence from Tabitha, but in that independence was a fierce loyalty to her family by blood and family by choice, which now included James. An outsider looking at Cassandra would see absolute contentment, a contentment that only comes from being in 'ultimate' love and knowing it was completely returned. James meanwhile being the steadfast gentleman would give everything he had for his family. And that family as of 24 hours ago had grown to include the four at this table even though at the time, he hadn't met three of them yet.

As a group, what most people saw was a family that would help anyone though anything at any time, for as long as any one of them lived.

The excitement of Marco's show slowly dissipated. Some of the other diners still watched, caught up by the feeling of love and camaraderie that exuded from the restaurant and staff. Of those who watched, a few were regulars, comfortable with the love and friendship that radiated from the restaurant and more would soon become regulars. The rest of the watchers were people who would never return because of the very reason others would.

"Okay. Okay now that the engagement is out, we still need to get to know you. You said you had three sisters and there are roughly twenty people for Christmas. Who are the other seventeen?" Tabitha wondered.

"Well there are my parents, Ron and Sharon, my brothers-in-law and all the kids. Monique is married to Kyle and they have four kids: Robbie, Jonas, Michaela, and Connie. Then there's Sam who's married to Renée. She's the middle sister. They have two kids, Jason and Sasha. Michelle is divorced and has no kids, but she and her high school sweetheart, Tom, got together again a few months ago after he found out she'd left Tom and I just found out they are engaged. Hmm, wait, six, four, well I guess twenty's a bit high, but there are still a lot of us and there's time and room to grow."

Monica said, "Yes, there is some growing now." She had a far off look in her eyes as she spoke. Her voice sounded weird, too. Grace gently nudged her. She snapped back, shook her head and grouched "What did I say this time?"

"Nothing, dear, just that it seems James is to be an uncle again."

"Oh good. I hate the doom and gloom ones."

"Us too, love," Tabitha chimed in. "Too boring coming from Goth girl. Much more fun from Composure girl here," pointing to Grace.

"YOU TWO STOP IT RIGHT NOW! You're scaring the normal again."

"It's okay, Grace. I can tell they need to fight as much as they need to breathe, just like you need to soothe."

"Yes, I suppose that is very true of us all."

"I have three sisters, remember? I know."

"I bet you do."

"It was hell growing up with them - four women, two men and never enough bathrooms. We could have all had our own and there wouldn't have been enough."

"Dad and I ended up taking a lot of cold or lukewarm showers over the years. He said a couple of years ago that it had been heaven taking hot showers instead of freezing his nipples off," James chuckled.

"Kind of a weird one for a man to use," Tabitha spoke up.

"Not really. The way Mom and Dad's shower is built; the water hits him right at his chest, so he has to duck to wash his hair. They are remodeling the house and that's the first thing he says is changing."

"Okay," Tabitha said understanding.

"What does your family do?" Grace continued the conversation.

"Hm. Mom's the elementary school secretary, Dad works for the utility company."

"What about your sisters?"

"Monique is staying home with the kids right now because it would cost more than she could make for the daycare, but prior to that she had been an office manager for one of the big legal offices. You know, keeping the lawyers staffed with admins and interns to look up stuff."

"Oh, cool."

"Renee works with Sam at The Packaging Store."

"Huh?" Cassandra asked confused.

"UPS Brown store. He owns it and she manages it now. Michelle is taking a course in spa management - learning how to run them and everything. Her fiancé, Matthew, is a fire fighter."

"What does Monique's husband do?"

"Landscape design. He does the eco-friendly stuff, where he only uses indigenous species and drought resistant plants when he can."

"I like him already."

"You'd love him. He's a nature fanatic, hybrid driving poster boy for Earth First!"

"A man after my own heart."

"Hey, your heart is mine."

"Didn't say he could have my heart."

"Alright, I'll let it slide."

"So no family business then?"

"No, not really. We all went our own ways, but we are still pretty tight. I think it helps that we don't see each other all day every day. I think there would be mass murder if we did."

"Oh."

Just then, Miguel brought their food out and conversation died down as food took over everyone's attention.

"What time will we see you Saturday, sweet?" Grace asked as they were getting ready to leave.

"I don't know, Aunt Grace, Yvette's here, but I don't know for how long. I need to ask her what's up."

"Ok, give us a call." Grace, Tabitha, and Monica kissed Cassandra.

"What's up with Saturday?"

"We get together and watch movies and eat food that is bad for us like chocolate and just have a day."

"You do this every Saturday?"

"No, just as often as we need it."

"Oh, so it's a girls' day."

"No. Mark came sometimes. Tabitha has brought boyfriends...usually it was for inspection and to see if they would pass muster, which they never do."

"Harsh bunch."

"No, just high standards."

CHAPTER NINTEEN

James felt a tingle of fear. Where did he fit in those standards? Was he even close? Cassandra's family was all free-spirited and new agers. Hell, she was a witch. Her aunts worked together curing the world, one person at a time.

"James, are you ok?"

"Huh? Yeah, I'm fine. Let's go."

"Ok. Why don't you drop me off at my apartment and I'll follow in a bit. I need to feed Freyja and get some clothes for work and some food for Odin."

"All right."

"Are you sure you're ok?"

"I said I'm fine." Cassandra knew better. James was forgetting she could feel his emotions and they were anger, envy and jealousy.

"Okay, then we'll go."

Neither said anything on the way to Cassandra's apartment. She leaned over and kissed him on the cheek when he pulled in front of her door. James barely noticed. "I'll see you in a few."

"Sure, okay, fine."

Cassandra's skin bristled from the emotions pouring from James. She decided she would let him

Cassandra's Heart

have the time it took her to get to his house before she would beat out of him whatever was bothering him.

"Hello Psycho, time for dinner. So, what do you think about this, Freyja? I know you know what's going on. Why don't you let me in on what's going through that man's head? The cat only sat staring at her mistress, "You are so damn annoying," Cassandra filled the cat's dry food bowl. "Fine, I'll be back in the morning. I have to go talk to the pain in the ass and find out why he's being such a jerk," She walked to her room, picked her clothes for the next day and grabbed shampoo and other toiletries. "See you in the morning, brat."

Cassandra drove towards James's house, but her mind was more on his reaction at dinner than her driving. Cassandra was so lost she didn't put together that the lights coming toward her were on her side of the road. She thought she heard a voice call her name but was too distracted. She just kept trying to figure out why James would lie to her about being upset. She had felt his anger and jealousy. The most confusing thing was the jealousy. It just didn't add up. Who could he have been jealous of? Cassandra shook her head thinking she heard her name again. She just kept replaying the evening in her mind, trying to see whom or what had caused James' anger. Damn it, this idiot needs to turn off his bright lights. She flicked her head light

137 | P a g e

up then down. "Oh fuck!" She shouted as she came out of her fog, there was a semi-truck in her lane and there was nowhere for her to go. She laid on her horn hoping to wake the driver in time. "Oh God, what the hell am I going to do!" At the last second, the driver did wake up and swerved into his own lane. He slammed on his brakes and skidded to a stop. Cassandra did the same thing. She laid her head on her steering wheel trying desperately to get her breathing under control. "Oh God, Oh God, Oh God, oh God."

"Ma'am are you ok? Oh man, please be ok."

"I'm fine, just shaken."

"I'm so sorry. Damn it, oh man."

"You should have stopped sooner, huh."

"There's a huge turnout up ahead I was going to stop there. This road is so narrow I couldn't stop before that."

"How far is it?"

The driver looked around to figure out where he was, "About half a mile, ma'am. I'm awake enough to make it to town now, but I won't. You're sure you're OK?"

"Yes, I'm sure. I'm only going a little farther down the road. I'm going to my fiancée's house."

"Okay. You can bet I'll be more careful in the future."

"How far over are you for your time?" Cassandra asked, referring to the limit truckers are supposed to drive.

"That's just it - I'm not. I'm an hour short, just too long of a road of nothing. Made my eyes tired looking at nothing and that did me in, I guess."

"So we're both OK then."

"Yes ma'am, I'm fine."

"Then I'm going to head on to my fiancés house."

Cassandra drove down the road leaving the still shaken driver to head towards town. Cassandra heard a whisper next to her. She turned instinctively towards the empty seat to see who it was but flushed while she did knowing she was in the car alone. Shaking her head and rubbing her hand over her face, she concentrated again on the road before her. "Cass... ca...ssan...Cassandra...Cassandra."

"What the hell?" Cassandra said aloud, "Damn, didn't know sleepiness was contagious. I must be daydreaming or something."

"Cassandra, you know you're not," replied the whispering voice.

"Shit! Shit! Shit!" Cassandra shouted and slammed on her brakes skidding to a halt just before James' driveway. In the seat next to her was a woman with bright blue eyes and golden blond hair who wore the most beautiful sarong style dress.

"What...who...what...?"Cassandra sputtered.

"In your heart I know you recognize me."

"But how?"

"You called."

"I did?" Cassandra said raising an eyebrow quizzically.

"Yes, you did."

"I called for you a year ago."

"A year ago you didn't really want me, you just wanted to use the motions of calling for me to get through the pain; a year ago you weren't ready for me."

"You could have fooled me."

"Yes, I could have, which is why I didn't come a year ago."

"So why are you here today? I haven't called you today."

"Do you really think you have to have a ritual to call me?"

"No."

"Well then, you have been asking me questions all night, and I thought I would answer them for you. Yes, yes, no, yes, no and 42."

"42, what question could be answered with 42?"

"The answer to the universe is 42." The goddess answered quoting The Hitchhiker's Guide to the Universe.

"Didn't realize I was asking that."

"Yes, and darling, you do really love James and you're right for each other. Did you truly love Marcus? You should go to girls' night and last, no you shouldn't worry about James, it will work itself out tonight."

"I didn't love Mark?"

"You did, but not the life time love you feel for James. Marcus was not meant for you to love for a lifetime."

"He wasn't?"

"No, my child, he wasn't; he was for another, and when I get Cleo again I'm going to skin her alive for the fun of it."

"Cleo."

"Cleopatra to you, and yes, that Cleopatra."

"You mean Marcus is…"

"Yes, he was from Rome. That's why…"

"He was so interested in all things Roman."

"Yes he missed home. He never put it together during this lifetime. Sometimes he does. Cleo always figures out she's Egyptian."

"Oh, OK, so now what?"

"You go up that drive and fight for what is yours."

"What is mine, James?"

"Yes, love."

"Freya, am I…"

"Are you what?"

"Am I yours?" Unsure of her thoughts, Cassandra whispered.

"Always, you're always mine, forever and always."

"Not like Cleo and Marcus?"

"No, you're mine." Freya laid her hand on her stomach. "You are from my line.

Marcus and Cleopatra came from mortals. They must move on through all the religions to find the place that is for them. As it turns out, in the end Marcus will always be for Janus and Cleopatra will always be for Ra because they never forget where they come from."

"Oh, okay I guess."

"You will understand some day, my love, trust in that."

"I do."

"So are you ready for your battle with James?"

"I don't know. I'm not much of a fighter."

"Oh yes you are!" Freya said when she was able to talk again after bursting in to laughter.

"Glad I could make you laugh, my lady."

"See, you are a fighter. You, my dear, have gone to Fólkvangr more valiantly then any of my other Valkyries, and more times, too, I might add. However, in this life you decided to carry a different shield and sword; words and love.

You decided you wanted to try something other than a warrior's life. It suits you, I would say."

Cassandra was completely baffled by that answer and asked, "Really?"

"I never kid, my little one."

"No, you were never the Trickster. That was always for Loki and Thor to goof around. So do I go bash him or seduce him?"

"You follow your heart and your instincts. They will let you know what to do. They have never led you down the wrong path and they never will."

"Hmm, well then I think a little bash to be followed by some seduction to smooth the hurt of the bashing. Don't suppose you would let me in on why he's so angry?"

"No fagur, I won't. That you will need to figure out for yourself. It should help you to decide what path to follow, but for now, you need to go. Someone is trying to take your head yet again."

CHAPTER TWENTY

"What!?" Cassandra's head whipped around and saw another set of headlights in her lane.

"Oh shit." Once more, she laid on her horn and flashed her lights. Cassandra floored her car and swerved into James' driveway. The other driver missed her bumper by inches after waking in the wrong lane and swerving into the proper lane.

Cassandra was shaken and upset when she pulled up in front of James' house.

She sat in her car a moment trying to regain some composure before the fight.

James had seen her pull up. He had been watching for her from his bedroom. He was trying to psych himself up for what he felt he needed to do. After hearing her talk about girls' night and how her family worked, he just didn't
know how they would ever combine to make one happy family.

Cassandra came up the steps but paused with her hand on the doorknob; she could feel the anger and pain. Odin greeted her at the door, and she knelt down to give her little king a hug. "Are you thirsty? Didn't he give you any water?" She walked the few steps to the kitchen and started opening cupboards. She found a large plastic butter tub. She filled it then set it down on a few paper towels. "Hey, those are my dishes. What do you think you're doing?"

"Giving my dog some water." Cassandra tried to keep her voice steady, in the end it cracked.

"What's with you?" he demanded angrily.

"Nothing, but what crawled up your ass sideways and died?"

"Look, nothing. I was just realizing on the way home that we are completely different and it would never work. The sex is great, but we are too different."

"Really?"

"I don't know what to say, Cassandra, we are just so..."

"Different." she finished for him. "James," she said as she walked him backwards towards the couch, "sit down and shut up." With a small shove, he lost his balance and flopped down on the suede couch.

"Cassandra, this won't change a thing."

"What part of shut up did you miss? I have had a very crazy twenty-four hours. I met the man of my dreams, literally; we have wild monkey sex several times. You met my coworkers and passed that test, not that it would have mattered. You met my family and passed that test, too, and that would have only slightly mattered. You asked me to marry

you and go home with you for Christmas; you brought me to your beautiful home where I reconnected with a
friend I've missed. I saw Freya and was almost hit head-on. Not once but twice to get out here so that you can dump me. I don't think so. This is nuts. What's this bull shit about our families not matching?"

"What do you mean almost hit twice? What are you talking about?"

"No, no changing the subject. You were trying to dump me."

"Cassandra, why were you in two almost-head-on collisions?" James's voice got louder with each word, his heart rate sped up to the point of causing him pain.

"James."

"Cassandra!"

She could tell he wasn't going to budge. "Just before the bridge, a truck driver nodded off and was in my lane. He woke up in time and pulled into his lane. He stopped, we talked, he was going on to a wide spot he knew about half a mile down the road, and no, he wasn't over his time, just tired from a boring section of road. Then Freya popped up and we talked a few minutes, and then some other idiot tried to run into me and hit my rear bumper and when I swerved into your driveway, he pulled back into his lane."

James leapt from the couch knocking Cassandra backwards he grabbed her and pulled her to his chest. "Oh my God, oh my God."

"James you can't be upset - you're dumping me."

James went still. 'Crap' he thought. "Cassandra just because I don't think we can have a permanent relationship doesn't mean I don't care and that I want to see you hurt."

"Well at least you aren't lying to me about that."

James pulled back to see Cassandra's face. "What are you talking about?"

"James, I'm an empath, remember? I feel what you feel. I knew you were angry at the restaurant. I knew you were still angry when I pulled in and until I mentioned the almost-accidents there was nothing but anger and hurt. Why the hurt? What had I said to cause you enough pain to make you re-evaluate our relationship already?"

Cassandra absently patted Odin's head while she waited for James to answer.

James turned away from her and walked to the kitchen. His mouth suddenly felt like he had swallowed several cotton balls. "Cassandra, you know what I said is true: we are very different, your aunts are triplets."

"So they are very different."

"But they are still triplets, ones who are trying to heal the world. You have a small family and mine at times feels like a small nation."

"None of that has anything to do with you being angry at Marco's."

"Look it doesn't matter. It won't work. You can take the bed. I'll sleep down here, in the morning you can go home."

"I am home, James."

James stopped short. He had been pouring a beer into a glass. "Shit!" he shouted as the foam over filled the glass "Damn it."

"James, I'm home and I'm not going to let you push me away, so just give it up. I'm not leaving."

"Cassandra."

"James, what pissed you off?"

"Nothing, alright? Nothing!"

Cassandra thought for a few minutes trying to remember the conversation just before he got mad. "Wait, wait, why would girls' night make you mad?"

"It doesn't, it's just another reason we would never last."

Cassandra could feel the anger and pain pulse from James. She wondered if he would ever know how much his pain hurt her, physically hurt her. "James, you idiot, you can't remember what I just told you?"

He looked at her, trying to figure out her game or angle or whatever. "I told you I'm empathic. I can FEEL your emotions. You are angry and hurt. I can also feel when you're lying to me."

"Cassandra, please just understand, we are too different."

"You keep saying the same thing, but you're not giving any examples."

James was crumbling, looking at her, he knew if he touched her he would never be able to walk away from her, but they really did have nothing in common.

Cassandra decided it was time to stop fighting and start seducing. He had sat back down on the couch again, so she stepped between his legs and then bit her tongue to keep from laughing when he jumped.

She leaned down, rubbed her hand up his thigh then back down again. "James, I think you really love me, but there is something holding you back. Why don't you relax and tell me what it is that is bothering you."

"I told you, we are just too different."

"Tell me the differences, James, tell me." Cassandra all but purred his name.

"Cassandra, I can't do this; you have to go."

"No I don't. I'm where I belong and you know it."

'Why was I mad at her?' James wondered. 'I know there was a reason, damn it. She's like a damn drug - once it's in your system you're screwed.'

"James, darling, love, why are you mad about girls' night?"

"Yeah, girls' night. The test."

"Yes it is. Why you are mad about it?"

"Cassandra, I would never pass muster; we are too different."

"You keep saying that, but James, you big dope, you already passed long before girls' night was mentioned. My aunts wouldn't have invited you to dinner if you hadn't passed."

"What?"

"You passed before my aunts left my apartment; also, I don't let them choose my men for me."

"But, but, what? I'm confused. You said that Tabitha and Monica bring over their dates for inspection and they never last."

"They don't last, you block head, because my aunts have never fallen in love with anyone. Tabitha is into airheaded men who can barley write their names.

She wants brains and brawn. She hasn't found it yet, that's all."

"So you guys don't tell each other to break up with your dates."

"Christ, no James, are you nuts?"

"Maybe."

"You are one of the cutest, craziest men I've ever seen, though."

Cassandra sat straddling James. "So do I get to meet your family now, do I pass muster?"

"You always have. I, I was just so scared that I wouldn't because I'm not a warlock or whatever."

"Honey, if you were a warlock you wouldn't have...it means oath breaker."

"Oh okay, but see your family would know that kind of stuff; mine won't."

"No one knows that kind of stuff because it's shown wrong in Hollywood."

"Well that's true."

"Look, I'm not letting you tank this relationship because you're scared."

"I'm not scared, I'm realistic."

"No, you're terrified. I can feel it."

James sat up a bit in the couch and bit the inside of his cheek to keep from telling Cassandra he wasn't terrified of the relationship, he was terrified of succeeding in making her leave.

Cassandra was still straddling his lap and she could feel his hard cock; hard and throbbing against her pussy. Sliding off his lap before he caught onto what she was going to do.

"No, no, no, we are not making love."

"James Austin, we are going to make love, because you dope, you love me, and I love you."

"No, Cassandra."

"James if you didn't love me for all of eternity, you would have said we weren't having sex, and to top it off you wouldn't have been hard, so it would be a moot point."

"Oh, well when you put it that way, the bedroom's upstairs, second door on the right."

ABOUT THE AUTHOR

Yasmina Kohl is a veteran writer with multiple titles already under her belt. Yasmina began writing romance novels and stories at the young age of 13 years old. Obviously, writing has always been a passion of hers and it has blossomed into a colorful career. Yasmina has an expertise in erotica writing and already has a published and printed series entitled "The Magical Ways Series". Currently, "The Magical Ways Series" has five released books and Yasmina plans to conclude the series after another two books. The sixth book is planned for release at the end of August, 2014. Yasmina exudes talent and creativeness. In addition to writing her erotica series, Yasmina is also the illustrator and designer of all her book covers. She has had the honor of being a featured author on TowerBabel.com, which is a website that connects readers to some of the top books on the market. A book series isn't enough for Yasmina though. She also is the President of the non-profit organization, "Waves of Words". This organization helps local and upcoming authors gain popularity and acknowledgment across the country. Being President is no small task, but Yasmina thoroughly enjoys helping others succeed and will do everything in her power to help make that goal a reality.

Follow YasminaKohl on Twitter, Facebook, Shelfari, Linkedin, Blogger, Librarything, Wordpress and Goodreads. Follow Yasmina Kohl on Twitter, Facebook, Shelfari, Linkedin, Librarything, and Goodreads. The user name for all the sites is yasminakohl.

Or drop her an email and let her know what you think at yasminakohl@gmail.com.

14313603R00088

Made in the USA
San Bernardino, CA
22 August 2014